I0618429

ABOUT THE AUTHOR

LESLIE FORD has become one of the most widely read mystery writers in America. Her first novel was published in 1928 and since then she has written over fifty others.

Miss Ford lives in Annapolis, Maryland.

Among her books are FALSE TO ANY MAN, OLD LOVER'S GHOST, THE TOWN CRIED MURDER, THE WOMAN IN BLACK, TRIAL BY AMBUSH, ILL MET BY MOONLIGHT, THE SIMPLE WAY OF POISON, THE CLUE OF THE JUDAS TREE, THREE BRIGHT PEBBLES, WASHINGTON WHISPERS MURDER, THE BAHAMAS MURDER CASE, THE PHILADELPHIA MURDER STORY, MURDER IS THE PAY-OFF, BY THE WATCHMAN'S CLOCK, MURDER IN MARYLAND, RENO RENDEZVOUS, INVITATION TO MURDER, and MURDER COMES TO EDEN, all published in Popular Library editions.

LESLIE FORD
ROAD TO FOLLY

WILDSIDE PRESS

Road to Folly

Published by Wildside Press LLC
www.wildsidepress.com

1

Phyllis Lattimer slipped a few inches further down on her elegant spine and lifted her jodhpurred feet neatly if inelegantly to the Villa Margherita's gleaming white balustrade.

"It doesn't matter what I want them for," she said. "I want them, and you're going to get them for me, darling. *That's* that I asked you down for."

I started to say something . . . I don't remember what.

"Look, Diane.—Strawberry Hill hasn't been touched. It's going to rack and ruin. You remember I tried to buy it when I bought Darien."

"And the old chatelaine wouldn't sell," I said. I remembered all of it. "Is she still alive?"

Phyllis nodded. "She's eighty-two, and she still won't sell. But that's not bothering me. I'll get it some day. It's what's *in* the house that I want . . . and that I'm going to get if it kills me."

"I see," I said.

She tossed her cigarette over the white balustrade into the masses of purple and pink and yellow stock and flame-colored snapdragons, and sat silently for a moment, a hard little line creasing the corners of her soft mouth.

"Diane," she said. "—That place is full of utterly priceless Charleston pieces! I've seen the inventory, and the bill. There's a ribband back Chippendale settee and eight chairs made by Simms in his shop in Queen Street. It's supposed to be like the settee the Boylstons have in New York—you've seen that. And just think of eight chairs *and* a settee! They're in the downstairs drawing room. And there's a satinwood secretary that's better than the Charleston one in the Cleveland Museum. My dear, it's a treasure house!"

Then, as if conscious that the set of her pointed jaw and the line of her scarlet mouth were too obstinately determined to be attractive, she turned her full face toward me and smiled.

"Don't go stuffy and . . . well, Charleston on me, my pet, will you?" she said lightly.

An elderly obviously Boston Back Bay dowager with a malacca stick, an obese Pekinese and a face of virgin granite, coming up the steps between the high white columns of Charleston's most exclusive caravanserie, glowered at her neat slim legs, at her feet profaning the white stone, and turned a perfect cyclamen red. Phyllis waved her hand airily without removing her bespoke English boots.

"Tourists utterly ruin Charleston, Diane. You wouldn't believe how enchanting it is before the season . . . and how unutterably foul it is during it."

The Back Bay voice grated pure corduroy. "—Who *is* that young woman? Is she stopping here?"

Pinckney, the Villa's hall boy with the soft warm voice, grinned as he took the ancient Pekinese. "No'm, *she* ain' stayin' here. She Miz' Russell Lattimer. She owns Darien Plantation."

The old lady grunted. "Oh. Oh, yes. Philadelphia." Even the screen door closed with a mollified thump.

Phyllis raised her shiny perfectly arched black brows and twisted one corner of her red mouth in a faintly ironic smile.

"So *anything's* quite all right, you see, Diane."

I looked at her. "It can't be very comfortable though, actually. Or doesn't that matter if it annoys the tourists enough?"

She groaned. "Lord, I knew you'd be difficult. That's why I didn't take time to change—so I could tell you about Strawberry Hill before anybody else got hold of you and headed you off."

"But if they don't want to sell their furniture, darling," I began.

"Oh, that's stupid," Phyllis said sharply. "It isn't 'they' in the first place, it's old Miss Caroline Reid. The chatelaine, as you call her. Which is just what she is, because she owns every stick of it, the plantation and the Charleston house too. She's the one who won't sell. Her daughter-in-law Mrs. Atwell Reid . . . she'd give her head to unload the whole business."

"But if it doesn't belong to her . . ."

"It does, really. I mean, to her and her two children, Colleton and Jennifer. They're not children, of course. Colleton's twenty-eight and Jennifer's twenty-two. Colleton lives in town with his mother, Jennifer's stuck out there at Strawberry Hill with old Miss Caroline—she not only won't sell, she won't move in to town. It just doesn't make sense, darling. I don't think people have any right to ruin other people's lives just because they hold the purse strings."

I glanced at her. For any one who had as strong a sense of the power that comes from holding the purse strings, it was as sardonic as it was inconsistent. But Phyllis was blissfully unaware of it, concerned only with justifying her own ends. Which was unusual. The only justification she'd ever needed in all the years I'd known her was that Phyllis wanted it and Phyllis was going to have it.

"Well, I suppose you'll explain, eventually," I said, with patience.

Phyllis Lattimer and I had been born and brought up next door to each other in town and country, and went to school together. I'd been a bridesmaid at her first wedding, and gone through a modified inferno with her family when she decided to divorce to marry Brad Porter. Bradley was handsome, well born, well connected, completely charming and totally worthless. Everybody knew it, even Phyllis until the day she decided to marry him. I'd been in at the death on that too, after it had lasted three years. In fact, it was Brad I'd felt sorry for then . . . just the sheer pace of trying to keep up with Phyllis had begun to put some iron into his soul. Then she met Rusty Lattimer, who was as different from Brad, and the people they tore from North to South to Europe to South America with, as any one could imagine. Meantime I'd married an architect, and when '32 came I did what so many young women had done who hadn't any training except that they'd been brought up with old furniture and had been to the Flea Fair in Paris, and turned decorator.

Phyllis and Brad's place in Middleburg was my first job, their house on Long Island my second, their ranch house in Wyoming my third, and when she divorced Brad in Reno and bought Darien Plantation on the Ashley near Charleston, I did that too. She'd met Rusty Lattimer one January when she and Brad were down in Charleston shooting wild turkey at a plantation near Walterboro. That was when she decided to marry him . . . without either his knowledge or consent. Just why was a little hard to figure out—or maybe not. He was frightfully good looking, blond with crisp sunburned hair and serious grey eyes and a hard lean suntanned face. Brad Porter was suntanned too, but too flabby from too much ease. Rusty's family was Charleston's finest and oldest and probably poorest. He'd worked, and gone to the University in Virginia, and come back apparently with a passion for seeing the lush subtropical land of his native Low Country produce something beside wild turkey and quail and camellias. A New York millionaire with half a dozen or so plantations on the Ashepoo got interested too, and Rusty had a free hand and a lot of money, and was doing a pretty swell job of it when Phyllis met him there at lunch.

"I'm sick of men that do nothing all day," she said to me. "I've decided to buy a plantation and do something with it too."

She up and went to Reno, divorced Brad, came back to Charleston, bought Darien Plantation, built a house and persuaded Rusty to help her block out a farm. At that point I knew he hadn't the chance of the proverbial snowball. I kept wanting to tell him it was only a phase, that in six months

7

she'd be sick of it and they'd be off to Sun Valley or Rio or Cannes, just when the cabbages needed him most. But you can't tell people things like that . . . not with Phyllis gazing, starry-eyed, at a brand new tractor, anyway.

So she married him. And I'll never forget that morning the second year, when the hunt coursed a fox over some very special field of his and Phyllis said, "Oh Rusty, you're such a bore." After that I saw them oftener at Newport and in Florida, and saw the struggle dying in his sea-grey eyes. And when I asked him once about the farm he shrugged and said, "Oh, hell, what's the use.—Boy, two more scotch and sodas."

"Some day he'll break away from it," I thought, "and do something with his life besides this. He's much too swell, he's got more guts than the people he's with."

That's why I'd thought, as I flew down from Philadelphia, that it was just to be one more marital deathbed. Phyllis I knew would never change. Rusty I hoped would have found his star again, and not still count his life by the number of turkeys he'd bagged on the land his forefathers had sweated to reclaim from virgin wilderness. But I was wrong. Phyllis was apparently top of the world, just being her spoiled little predatory self, wanting a new version of the moon—new for her—and willing, apparently, to use fair means or foul to get it. And moreover expecting me, apparently, to get it for her. Because from everything I knew about Charleston, and Strawberry Hill Plantation, and the people who owned it, I knew she had—as my colored houseman says—taken more on her fork than she could eat.

"—The old South isn't weakening your moral fiber, by any chance, is it, darling?" I asked.

She laughed shortly and shook her head.

"No," she said. "But they're sort of funny, down here. You think everything's dandy, and you find yourself smack up against a stone wall. I think Pride is what it's called, or Honor maybe. It doesn't make sense either, and a lot of it's a sort of crumbly façade. But with the Reids it isn't crumbly at all.—It was Colleton that killed his father, you know."

I started in spite of myself. I wasn't even sure I'd heard correctly.

"That *what?*"

She looked at me as if I was the one who was being surprising.

"You remember, Diane. I told you. You met him with us in Newport. The tall awfully dark chap with black eyes that shot his father when he was fifteen."

I shook my head. "It was somebody else."

"No, no! The one that's mad about Rusty's sister—Anne

8

Lattimer. Only he won't ask her to marry him because of the stigma."

She shrugged. "Although since when murder's stigmatic in Charleston is something I wouldn't know."

"Meaning?"

"All I know is what I read in the papers. There was an editorial in the paper just a little while ago asking when murder had been considered a capital crime in South Carolina . . . no white man of property had been executed for something like forty-six years, and that was a departure from the norm or something. I'm rather vague about it."

"It's the sea air, probably," I said. "Vague is the one thing I'd have sworn you never were—about anything."

"Perhaps not. Anyway, that's what we'll call it. And that's the way it is—I mean about Colleton Reid. He shot and killed his papa, who apparently was something, even for down here. It was out at Strawberry Hill."

Then the memory of the day in Newport two years before came back to me . . . of a dark young man whose eyes kept following Anne Lattimer, Phyllis's quite lovely but I thought definitely unhappy sister-in-law, around the room with such naked living hell in them that I finally asked Rusty what was wrong. And I got a polite but potent rebuff that I didn't forget for days. Phyllis, however, had been communicative enough.

"But you said he'd lost his father, he'd been accidentally killed when he was cleaning his gun after a neighborhood deer hunt."

"That's what Rusty told me. That was before I knew how euphemistic people here are about such episodes."

"Oh," I said.

"It's natural enough, I suppose, in a community as tight as this."

Phyllis shrugged her slim tweed shoulders again.

"Of course, Rusty could get the stuff for me if he wanted to, but he won't. He's absolutely forbidden me to even try to get it, or try to get the old woman off Strawberry Hill. He seems to think it doesn't matter how poor they are, they ought to keep what they've got.—Jennifer, she's old Miss Caroline's great-niece, has got the same crazy *idée fixe* about the land Rusty has. She's the one really that won't sell the furniture."

She smiled, tapping her foot. "But I've got Brad working on her. I'll show Rusty he's not as smart as he thinks."

There's no reason, these days, I suppose, why an ex-husband shouldn't be on tap, but I was surprised nevertheless.

"Brad?" I said. "Is he around?"

"Off and on," she said shortly. Then after a moment she

added, "He's kept us in quail this winter. Rusty's gone native."

Going native in the Carolina Low Country would seem to have so many possibilities that I didn't attempt to figure it out. I just waited. Phyllis had put one foot up on the edge of her chair seat and was sitting with her strong brown hands clasped around her knee, staring out between the white fluted columns above the palmetto trees into the blue cloudless space.

"Rusty, my pet, has returned to agriculture," she said, after a long silence. "I thought I'd got it out of his system, but back it's cropped like a rash.—It's unsocial, or something, to have a lot of land and not do something with it. I'd think it was Jennifer's influence, but he never goes over there."

She yawned.

"It's too tiresome. I'd got him practically civilized . . . now I've got to begin all over again. But I've really got him stymied now. It costs money to farm—and fortunately it's *my* money."

The little creases in the corners of her mouth hardened. If it hadn't been for them she wouldn't have looked twenty-five. With them she looked more thirty-five than thirty.

"I thought you didn't think the people who held the purse strings had a right to dictate to other people," I said.

"This is different. I'm not going to stay down here till the middle of July and get malaria just for the sake of having Rusty spend all day in the barn bringing up Guernsey cows, or sitting up all night worrying whether the frost is killing the young cabbages. My God."

"I thought you married him because you were tired of men who did nothing all day," I observed.

She shrugged. "I thought it would be amusing to be a gentleman farmer. I didn't know it was twenty-four hours a day twelve months a year. Anyway, I'm sick of it, and I'm sick of Rusty. What the hell do I care about his cows and his cabbages, and whether a lot of Negro farm hands have a pig and chickens or not? I'm bored stiff with the whole business. I'm not going to let Rusty disrupt my whole life."

I started to say, "Then why don't you go to Reno again?" but I didn't.

All the airy gaiety had gone out of her face. The grim determination of a gal who'd always had her own way had hardened in it.

"Let's skip it, shall we?"

She glanced at me, trying to recapture the earlier mood. I nodded.

"Okay. Let's go back to Strawberry Hill," I said. "Where do I come in the picture? That's what I can't make out."

"It's very simple. More than that, it's a natural, really. You will do it, won't you?"

"It depends," I said. It wouldn't be the first scheme of Phyllis Lattimer's that I'd been uneasy about, nor would it be the only one I'd walked out on.

"I mean, Diane, it isn't just that you'll be doing me a favor. It'll be an act of kindness to everybody. It really will. Wait till you see Jennifer and Colleton. You'll see exactly what I mean. And their mother too. It's a rotten shame—they really need the money."

I looked at her. It doesn't do to be too cold-blooded about one's friends, but I couldn't help it here.

"I know exactly what you're thinking," she said, with a shrug. "I admit I want the furniture. And if I don't get it before old Miss Caroline dies, I'll never get it. Because Jennifer will get it—every stick of it. That's why she guards the old woman like a watch dog.—And I want it, I tell you."

"Which obviously settles it," I said.

"It does as far as I'm concerned," she retorted curtly.

"Then why don't you go to Miss Caroline and explain it to her? She seems to be a rugged individualist too. She might understand you perfectly."

"Because she doesn't receive visitors, that's why," she answered, still more curtly. "That's the only reason in the world I don't. I've tried a thousand times. She doesn't allow anybody but about three blue-blooded octogenarian cousins from below Broad Street in the presence."

"What about Jennifer and Colleton and their mother?"

"They'd sell in a minute—Colleton and his mother, not Jennifer. She knows the old lady will die pretty soon, and she's in on the ground floor. I'm sure she's the stumbling block in the whole thing."

"Have you tried working on them?"

"—Have I."

She fished in her tweed jacket pocket and pulled out a cigarette.

"If I could only see old Miss Caroline," she said slowly. "That's all I need.—That's what I want you for."

I gasped at that. "Me?"

She nodded. "I just found out yesterday from Colleton's mother, and rushed out and wired you. You can do it—on two counts."

"You've got a touch of fever already, darling," I said patiently. "But do go on."

She glanced over her shoulder at the empty verandah. The brilliant afternoon sun going down beyond the Battery stencilled a moving arabesque of long palmetto leaves on the white columns and filtered across the closed door with its

11

great polished brass knocker. She put her feet up on the gleaming balustrade again and leaned her head nearer my chair.

"Old Miss Caroline visited your grandmother two winters in Philadelphia, in the Eighties. She was introduced to society with her, and they were presented at the Monday Germans in Baltimore together. Her mother had known your great-grandfather before the War—that's the Civil War, down here, you know. There's some connection there that explains why Strawberry Hill wasn't burned when Darien was, during the march to the sea. I haven't got it quite clear, but that's it. Anyway, the point is—she'll receive you."

"Oh," I said . . . rather stiffly.

Phyllis wouldn't notice that. She went blandly and blindly on.

"But wait. That's not all."

She took her feet down again and leaned forward, her pointed chin cupped in her brown palm.

"Miss Caroline, like everybody else down here, has written her memoirs . . . and also like everybody else, thinks that if she could find an honest publisher, she'd make a fortune. I heard Jennifer talking to a man about them the other day. And that's where both you and I come in."

I looked at her. There was a shrewd concentrated intentness in her face that was new to me, well as I knew her. I was a little angry, but I was interested. I couldn't help being. I knew of course that Phyllis could read; I never had known that she cared enough about people generally to know that they liked to write.

"Your brother is a publisher. I'll pay for a ghost to sort out the memoirs and have them published . . . as de luxe as hell. She'll love it."

A sardonic little smile crossed her eyes. "The rest will be pie. You know about people being motivated by vanity and cupidity. This is Miss Caroline's vanity against Mrs. Reid's cupidity. It's very simple."

"I'd skip it, Phyllis," I said.

She shook her head.

I shook mine.

"It stinks," I said coarsely.

She settled back in her chair, her brown face a little pale, her dark eyes smoldering.

"I always thought you were the one person in the world I could count on, Diane," she said. Her foot at the end of her crossed jodhpurred leg beat a tattoo on the white fat-bellied balustrade stretchers, the way an angry cat's tail moves against a chair leg.

"Be your age, Phyllis," I retorted, rather angry too. "It's just not the sort of thing people do."

12

We sat in silence—not, I may say, a particularly comfortable one—for several moments. The blue, almost Mediterranean sky above the palmettos and live oaks with their thin wisps of grey moss, the bluer water beyond and the low mauve line of the islands beyond it, the cool brilliant sun going down to meet them . . . these were Charleston, and another world. And not, moreover, a world in which one chiselled a great old lady out of the gods she clung to . . . not if one had any faith to keep.

"I'd be willing to pay almost anything, within reason," Phyllis said, after a long time. "More than any New York dealer would."

I don't know why that annoyed me more than anything she'd said.

"Maybe there are a few things your money can't buy, Phyllis," I said shortly.

She shrugged. "I've never seen one of them."

I realized that it was I who was being the stupider of the two. She never had, of course . . . because of the values she lived by. The things money didn't buy had never been the ones she'd happened to want before.

"I only said 'Maybe,' " I answered.

She put out her brown hand suddenly and took hold of my Northern-winter-white one.

"Oh, please, Diane, let's not quarrel," she said quickly. "It's just that I do so much want that stuff! I can't tell you why. Maybe I don't know myself."

"I do," I said. "It's because you're spoiled, and you can't bear not to have your own way. You don't actually give a damn about whether a piece of furniture is Chippendale or Grand Rapids, or was made in Charleston or in Timbuctoo—and you can't put your muddy riding boots up on a ribband back settee. You just want to prove your old saw about vanity and cupidity . . . and show your own superiority."

The tiny lines around her eyes tightened. I don't think Phyllis, however, had ever even tried to deceive herself—no matter how thoroughly she deceived anybody else. She sat silently a few moments. Then she said, "You know, I don't know why I let people like Rusty or Anne Lattimer, or even the Reids, make me feel . . . well, frustrated—but they do, some way. You can be as superior as you like about them. They haven't any money, they're sterile in lots of ways, and they're decadent. A lot of this pride and ancestor stuff is pride strained pretty thin. But they've got something the Northerners who come down and buy their plantations and become a lot of absentee landlords haven't got . . . and never do get. If they had it they'd stay at home. It's all an escape, and you don't try to escape if you're not frustrated, do you?"

13

"I don't know," I said.

"Oh, well, what the hell."

She got up and stood, her fingers stuffed into her jodhpur pockets. Then she turned around.

"Just remember—I'll pay for publishing the memoirs. Tell her that when you see her."

"I'm not seeing her, darling. Get that out of your head permanently."

Phyllis shrugged her tweed shoulders in their perfectly tailored brown-checked jacket.

"You're missing the chance of a lifetime, is all I can say."

She picked her hat up off the floor and put it on the back of her head.

"We're going out to dinner before the theatre tonight. Will you join us there?"

I shook my head.

"Then I'll send in for you tomorrow. You don't have to go if you don't want to . . . but even if you won't help me, you'll come out to Darien for a while, won't you?"

"I'll see," I said. "I ought to get back home."

She took an impulsive step toward me and pecked me on the cheek. "You've never really understood me, Diane," she said lightly. "Maybe I'm not really as bad as you think I am."

"Or maybe worse," I said.

"That's probably nearer the truth," she laughed. And I've wondered since whether she meant that, and if she hadn't even then seen further into what she would do, and even why she would do it, than I in my innocence did.

She ran down the broad steps of the Villa, and waved at me from her open car. I stood there a moment. Suddenly I shivered. It seemed quite cold. Maybe it was that the sun had dropped its red disc lower into the islands beyond the bay, so that the palmettos were almost purple and the shafts of light were golden arrows through the live oaks. Or it may have been the sudden eerie strum of a guitar that came to my ear. I looked along the street to where an old blind Negro was sitting under the oak tree in the parking strip, rolling his sightless eyes up to the sky.—Or it may have been the rich monotonous cadence of the line he was singing:

"When the moon goes down in blood . . ."

which was all I understood before I opened the door and went quickly into the Villa.

14

2

When I told Phyllis I wouldn't join them at the theatre that night I'd meant it. I'd seen about enough of her to last me a good week, for one thing. I'd also heard the Society for the Preservation of Spirituals sing a number of times, both here and in New York. I hadn't, however, counted on meeting an old friend of my mother's dining in solitary grandeur, just waiting to pounce on the first likely person to use her other ticket.

I'm sure now it was Fate itself, lurking in the clear green waters of the Villa pool. If I hadn't gone that night, I'd never have seen, in the kind of blinding clarity that a streak of lightning illuminates a countryside with, so that it sticks in your retina long after it's dark again, the situation that made an awful lot of things Phyllis had said, or not said, dreadfully clear and dreadfully important. Nor should I have had the exclusive—assuming that everybody within a mile of us was deaf—services of a super-commentator on the Charleston scene who by a dozen winters and a lot of relatives had picked up enough local gossip to make the recent tornado look like a summer zephyr.

She was leaving the next day, and I suppose it was that fact among others that unlocked the flood gates. Though in some ways there's an appalling lack of ordinary reticence about other people's affairs in Charleston, just as on the other hand there's also an even stronger code of "That's the sort of thing one doesn't discuss." It depends, I suppose, on which clan is discussing what . . . though again—and this really did amaze me—there was the most total silence, on the part of a very considerable and very dissimilar group of people, on a couple of points that would have seemed to an ordinary observer very legitimate subjects of gossip, that any one could imagine.

The odd thing about both of those points was that they weren't actually that important to anybody, and a lot of unhappiness and the lives of at least two people and perhaps a third would have been saved if the discussion had been nearly as free . . . well, as in another quite famous Charleston *cause celèbre*. But that's the sort of thing—its reticence and its lack of it, depending on the occasion—that seems to me part of the charm, and certainly part of the enigma, of Charleston.—How, for instance, a dozen people could sit Sunday after Sunday in St. Michael's and watch two of their

15

friends, their eyes fastened on the letters "Thou Shalt Do No Murder" burned in letters of gold on the cypress altar panel, and never breathe a word of it, still astonished me, a mere tourist.

It was a little late when we hurried through the reddish stone pillars of the first theatre in America. The jaunty little painted figures of the be-turbanned eighteenth century Negro pageboys, with their brocaded coats and lace jabots, holding the yellow cords in the foyer, were startlingly real for a moment. It was the first time I'd seen the restoration of the Dock Street Theatre, and I was delighted. The Society for the Preservation of Spirituals was singing "Eberybody Libin' Goin' to Die." It was very nice. The ladies in their full-skirted off-the-shoulder gowns didn't look the least ante-bellum, what with the present styles, but the gentlemen in their ruffled shirt fronts and black ribband ties did, very. And when the lights went up at the interval it seemed to me that all of Charleston not on the stage was on the floor.

I looked around.

"Look, my dear." My mother's friend nudged me violently. "That's Mrs. Atwell Reid . . . that lovely woman with the white hair."

We'd got up and were following a fair part of the audience out into the moonlit courtyard, with its high brick walls and the massed azaleas from Middleton Gardens just coming into bloom. It was quite all right to stop and stare around at people, because the Dock Street Theatre manages someway to combine the intimate quality of a neighborhood country club and an almost continental sophistication. I don't suppose any theatre that hadn't a genteel tradition stretching back to 1736, or that hadn't been restored as a community enterprise in the best sense, could possibly have quite the friendly feel of noblesse oblige that this one has.

"See . . . the woman with the tall young man."

My mother's friend nudged me again. It was the tall young man I was looking at. I remembered perfectly the tight lean jaw and the dark haunted eyes with shaggy brows making them seem more deeply set than they really were. And I wondered then, as I've wondered a good many times since, if murder doesn't take its own bitter toll when society doesn't. It had certainly set Colleton Reid apart. Phyllis's "No one ever asks him to shoot with them" flashed through my mind.

But it wasn't Colleton Reid, really, that I was interested in. It was the big blond-haired man following Phyllis Lattimer up the crowded aisle, head and shoulders above most of the people around him. Rusty Lattimer's face had lost the defeated, almost sullen look it had had when I saw him last in Palm Beach in a chromium and white leather chair under a yellow beach umbrella, a fifth or sixth whisky and soda

16

in his hand. His grey eyes were clear and hard, his face lean and brown and determined. He didn't, God knows, look happy, but he did look like a man who was captain of his soul.

My mother's friend touched my elbow. "That's her son, Colleton Reid.—Oh, how do you do, Mrs. Reid? This child is Diane Baker from Philadelphia.—And Mr. Reid."

Colleton and his mother gave me oblique greetings in the crowded aisle. Phyllis Lattimer, moving out into the courtyard, spotted me and nodded brightly. I had the uneasy feeling that her sharp little mind was busy every moment. And we'd no sooner crossed the foyer into the white moonlight than she was beside me, one hand on my wrist and the other on Mrs. Atwell Reid's.

"Diane—this is marvellous! How *did* you happen to turn up in Charleston? My dear, why *didn't* you wire me you were coming?"

She was turning on her full radiance, knowing I couldn't possibly do anything about it.

"This is Diane Baker, Mrs. Reid. We were talking about her yesterday . . . it was her grandmother Miss Caroline stayed with in Philadelphia."

Mrs. Reid, firmly pinioned by Phyllis's right hand, held out hers. She was tall, with snowy-white hair and clear fine skin, blue eyes and dark brows. She was over fifty, I suppose, and still gracefully slender in a grey lace dress with long sleeves, high neckline, and pearls around her throat. She was a stunning woman still, but I knew she must have been unbelievably lovely when she was young.

"You've been in Charleston before, haven't you?" she asked. "I've heard of you from time to time. I want you to meet my son."

She glanced around. Colleton Reid had moved away and was over by the fountain in the wall, talking to a blonde girl I recognized as Rusty Lattimer's sister Anne. She was much thinner and more tired-looking than when I'd met her at Phyllis's in Newport. Her hands were nervous; she smoked three cigarettes, it seemed to me, to Colleton Reid's one, and smiled too brightly at people as they moved back and forth.

"You know Rusty, Diane."

Phyllis released Mrs. Reid's arm and took hold of her husband's.

"*Hullo!* How did you get down here?"

Rusty Lattimer grinned and held out his hand. It was like taking hold of a piece of iron wrapped in coarse sandpaper.

"It's funny, Phyllis was talking about you last night . . . wondering if you'd given us all the go-by."

A flicker of anxiety went through his wife's face. For an instant I think she wasn't so sure I wasn't going to let her

17

down with a thud. She had it coming, I thought; but there was something in Rusty Lattimer's face now that I saw it closer that would have stopped me even if I'd been the gal to do it—which I wasn't, and which Phyllis, of course, knew very well. I had the instant feeling that Rusty Lattimer needed all the faith he had in his wife . . . even needed it bolstered as much as possible. There was a kind of profound disillusionment 'in the back of his grey eyes and in the sun lines at the corners of them, and in the almost grim set of his big mouth, that even his welcoming grin didn't manage to wipe out.

Just then, as I'd said, "Oh, I'm apt to turn up practically anywhere," the darnedest thing happened. There was one of those instants of silence that sometimes fall on a room full of chattering, laughing people, and a warm soft voice fell across it like sunlight through a glass of rich burgundy.

"Don't be *silly!*"

I don't know why particularly—because people can be silly about a lot of things—but the whole quality of it, the warmth, the laughing banter, a kind of rejection and at the same time invitation, with complete mastery of the situation, indicated as plain as day that a man was making love to a girl. And just as instantly every one in the group I was interested in stiffened like so much frozen meat. Because I was facing the wall I couldn't see the girl, but I saw the rest of them: Mrs. Reid's sudden panic of alarm, her son Colleton's eyes flashing dark fire. I saw the girl beside him give him a quick frightened glance as her eyes moved from him to his mother, and then to her brother.

And it was Rusty Lattimer's face that really stopped me. If anybody could translate visually, in anybody else's face, the kind of instant and gone but perfectly tormenting pain that shoots through a tooth you'd thought was perfectly sound, that would be the nearest approach to what I saw there. Rusty Lattimer was in love with this girl . . . and I knew she must be Jennifer Reid. I knew he was—instantly, clearly and definitely. I knew too that it was a destroying kind of love, and utterly hopeless, because Rusty was the kind of man who being married to another woman could do nothing about it.

I was literally stunned. It was the only thing I hadn't thought of coming down on the plane. It just simply had never occurred to me that a man Phyllis wanted could be in love with anybody else. I glanced at her, and stopped again. She was still smiling . . . untouched and completely confident, looking at her husband with an amused, almost mocking smile, it seemed to me. In fact she looked precisely like a prize cat that had not only won the blue ribbon but had got a saucer of thick yellow cream thrown in.

18

Then every one started talking again. It hadn't taken, all of it, more than a split second . . . but it was all there, a situation perched neatly on as large a keg of dynamite as I've ever seen in a public place.

I glanced around. A girl and a man were standing beside a tub of blush-pink camellias, beside the stone column under the long tiled stoop over the foyer doors. The girl, apparently unconscious of anything unusual, was laughing up at the man whose back was turned toward us. She was dark, with short cropped curly black hair, blue silvery black in the white moonlight. Her face and bare arms, and throat above her black net dress, were as warm as her voice and as cool as the camellias in the tree beside her, her eyes were blue and dancing. But it wasn't them, or her face or her skin, as much as some quality over and above all of them that made her electric just then.

Then the man turned, and if it had been a simple enough problem in dynamite before, I realized now that it was anything but. It was Phyllis's divorced husband, Bradley Porter. I looked at Phyllis. She gave me a quick almost imperceptible wink, and I felt my face flush angrily. It wasn't fair, and it wasn't decent. I was ashamed of Brad even more than of her, to let himself be part of her scheme to defeat anything so young and lovely, with such a proud little head and clear untarnished eyes.

And I looked at Rusty. Did he know, I wondered? Was that part of the disillusionment and racking pain behind his own clear eyes? I think I could have killed Phyllis just then. And I could see she knew very easily what I was thinking. She laughed suddenly.

"—Brad, darling!"

Her voice, warm and a little mocking, made him turn toward us. I saw the old charming light kindle in his eyes. It had kindled for all women, but quicker for Phyllis. I saw now that it still did, and I saw that Phyllis knew it did . . . and that she would use it when she needed it, let the chips fall where they might.

"Come here, Brad—here's Diane!" she called.

Brad Porter dislodged himself from against the stone column.

"Well, for God's sake!"

He piloted the girl across the flagged court, his hand out. I was watching her. The smile had gone out of her face the way the moon can go behind a fleece of white clouds, taking all the shimmering luminous glow out of the world.

"Phyllis was talking about you yesterday. I bet she knew you were coming, the rat."

"Brad, you beast!" Phyllis cried.

"I'll even bet she sent for you—didn't she?" ·

19

I laughed and shook my head.

"Watch out for dirty work at the crossroads," he said cheerfully. "Whenever Phyl's got a hot chestnut to pull out, she drags Diane in for front."

He pulled the girl closer to the group.

"This is Jennifer Reid . . . Diane Baker. Or have you met?"

Jennifer Reid didn't hold out her hand. She stood there in the very thick of us, and yet she gave, in some way that I couldn't put my finger on, the most extraordinary sense of being completely isolated from all of us, as if she were in the center of an empty stage. She didn't look at Rusty. She didn't even know, I thought, that he had turned away to keep from looking at her.

I glanced at her mother. She'd moved too, and was bowing formally to a man who'd been talking to another man near the open door of the foyer. He was bowing to her. My mother's friend caught my eye and went through an elaborate pantomime that I gathered meant I was to look at him carefully. When I did, I thought he seemed rather nice but not particularly exciting. He was large and heavy-set, with grey hair and a reserved strong-featured face, around sixty, I imagine, and not unattractive in a quiet self-contained sort of way.

Just then Mrs. Reid turned back to us, or rather to her daughter who'd moved over toward her. She kissed her cheek perfunctorily.

"We didn't know you were coming in, Jennifer," she said. The anxiety in her eyes touched her voice, and apparently asked another question without stating it. Jennifer said,

"Rachel is with Aunt Caroline. She said it was all right for me to come."

It seemed to me there was something a little rebellious in the girl's voice, and I thought defensive too. There certainly didn't appear to be any great warmth between mother and daughter. I thought of what Phyllis had said—that Jennifer was guarding all her aunt's property for herself, and wondered. Her mother seemed in some curious way annoyed that she was here.

Brad Porter, whose life has had a large piece of it devoted to getting around women of all ages, spoke up quickly.

"I hope you don't mind, Mrs. Reid." He turned on the well-known charm. "It's all my fault. I persuaded her to come."

Mrs. Reid looked at him, or rather through him, without a trace of cordiality. "I'm sure Jennifer felt she could leave her aunt quite comfortably, or she wouldn't have done it."

Jennifer's pale luminous face flushed, her eyes darkened. Just then, fortunately, the curtain bell rang, and men and women dropped their cigarettes on the flags or buried them in the camellia tubs, and moved back into the theatre. I didn't hear much of the second half of the performance. I was thinking about too many other things, and chiefly about the quick glance I'd seen pass between Phyllis Lattimer and her ex-husband Bradley Porter. Hers had been a question; he'd shaken his head, almost imperceptibly. Whatever she had wanted him to do, it was plain he'd not done it . . . not yet. And I was worried. What chance had Jennifer Reid with those two against her?

"Did you see the man Mrs. Reid was talking to?" my mother's friend asked avidly, as soon as her chauffeur had picked us up and started down Church Street toward the Battery. "Well, my dear, that's John Michener. Her husband was his first cousin. They both courted her. She was supposed to be in love with John, but Atwell Reid had the property and her mother was a bitter determined old woman."

We turned down East Bay.

"Well, my dear, John Michener and a party of men were just leaving the plantation after a deer hunt when they heard the shot, and they all went back and found Atwell Reid dead. Of course they hushed it all up, said he'd been putting up his gun. They sent Colleton north to school, you know, for a long time. Everybody thought they'd marry—John and Elsie Reid—as soon as it blew over. But they never have. Colleton loathes him, and Mrs. Reid's afraid of Colleton, and just as spineless now as when she let her mother dominate her. Everybody thinks if Colleton marries Anne Lattimer, then he won't care so much about his mother. Jennifer's charming, don't you think? They say she's responsible for old Miss Caroline staying out at Strawberry Hill, so she'll get all the lovely furniture some day. The house is full of it. They say she's the one that keeps the place shut up like a prison."

We drew up in front of the brilliant white-porticoed grandeur of the Villa.

"However, my dear," my mother's friend sighed, "you can see her mother doesn't want her going around with that attractive Brad Porter. I think it's ridiculous, myself, but you know how they are down here. They don't have divorce in South Carolina—it's the only state in the Union where they don't. And old Charlestonians don't approve of their daughters marrying divorced men. Especially divorced men who're dependent on their divorced wives' pocketbooks. And the Reids are as old Charleston as St. Michael's Well.—Thank you for going with me, dear. I hope you were amused."

As I undressed for bed it seemed to me that "amused" was someway not quite the word for it.

3

I'd forgot that people still make formal calls, in Charleston, and also that they do it in the morning. That's why I was a little surprised, and with my carry-over from the night before, a little dismayed, coming into the gold drawing room and finding Mrs. Atwell Reid and her daughter Jennifer sitting there. Mrs. Reid held out her hand cordially. Jennifer Reid's blue eyes met mine so coolly that I wondered why she'd bothered to come at all. Moreover, she didn't open her mouth while her mother and I went through the elaborate ritual of Charleston.—It was a beautiful city. The gardens were lovely, the food divine. It was snowing in New York, and rather colder in Charleston than it normally was at this time of year. How long was I staying, and had I been to the antique show at St. Philip's Rectory?

That over, Mrs. Atwell Reid glanced a little anxiously at her daughter, who sat in a gold-brocaded chair, her motionless face even lovelier in the brilliant daylight than it had been in the moonlight the night before. She had on a blue checked jacket and powder blue sweater and a little blue felt hat worn back from her high camellia-textured forehead, and if I hadn't known she was twenty-two I'd have thought she was about sixteen.

She didn't move now, but I knew she'd caught her mother's glance. The shuttered look in her eyes as she glanced down at her hands, folded primly in her lap, showed that plainly. And showed further that she was being forced into something definitely against her will. There was an awkward silence. I saw the corners of her red lips tremble. She looked up at me.

"I told Aunt Caroline you were here," she said quietly. There was still the warm soft note in her voice that Southern women have if their voices aren't high-pitched the way most of them are. "She would like you to come out to see her."

For a moment our eyes met . . . hers clear and young, and . . . not so much resentful, I thought, as challenging. Then her mother broke in.

"My aunt doesn't receive many people. She's quite old . . . she was eighty in December. She's almost blind on account of a cataract she stubbornly refuses to have operated on. But her mind is as clear as it ever was."

She said it rapidly, almost like a cataract herself.

"And that's very clear," Jennifer said coolly, still looking at me.

"Of course it is, Jennifer," her mother said hastily. "I didn't mean to imply it wasn't. I'm sure Mrs. Baker didn't think I did."

I looked at Jennifer. I had the uneasy feeling that I knew perfectly what she meant, even if her mother didn't. Had what Brad Porter said about my being Phyllis's front when there was dirty work at the crossroad meant more to her than any one had thought the night before?

"You will go out and see her, won't you, my dear?" Mrs. Atwell Reid said nervously.

I saw the shutters go down in Jennifer's eyes again, and I made up my mind permanently this time. This was one of Phyllis Lattimer's chestnuts that I was going to let religiously alone. I turned to Mrs. Atwell Reid.

"I'm so sorry! I'd have loved to." I said. "I'm awfully afraid I'm taking the afternoon plane home. I really just flew down to have a look at the Antique Show at St. Philip's, and I have to be back almost immediately."

The very mention of antiques was an awful mistake. Jennifer's face shut like a steel trap. She didn't look at her mother. So, I thought; she knows exactly what Phyllis Lattimer wants, and probably why she sent for me to come down. Knowing Phyllis, and hearing Brad the night before, even if he hadn't said anything to her later, she could easily have put two and two together. She obviously had, I thought . . . and had got a lot more than the traditional four.

She got up quickly. Her manner had changed abruptly to an easy rather than uneasy aloofness.

"Perhaps when you come again . . ."

But her mother hadn't risen. She was sitting erect and graceful, her face suddenly worn and tired as her daughter's freshened. She got up then, slowly, not looking—oh, definitely not looking—at Jennifer.

"Couldn't you take the late plane, Mrs. Baker? My aunt is really very anxious indeed to see you," she said, with a kind of gentle persistence that was very embarrassing. "You see, some one told her you might be down this winter. She's set her heart on seeing you."

"But, mother! If Mrs. Baker has to go home, it's unkind of you to put her in this position."

Jennifer Reid's voice was still warm velvet, but under it was something else. It wasn't just determination, either. It was fear, just plain paralyzing fear. I sensed it with the kind of intuitive clarity that makes rational processes slow and plodding. And I didn't look at her. I didn't want to. It was her mother I was concerned with. Why was she so insistent that I go to see old Miss Caroline at Strawberry Hill . . .

so insistent in the face of her daughter's desperate—it seemed to me now—determination that I should not that she was allowing a formal morning call on a complete stranger to become practically an emotional scene?

Just then a girl I didn't know wandered into the card room.

"Jennifer Reid! How perfectly swell! I was going to look you up . . . I've got a husband, I want you to see him! Jim!! —Where *has* he got to?"

And in the gay confusion I felt Mrs. Atwell Reid's hand on my arm, and heard her voice entreating me hurriedly:

"My dear . . . please go out to see my aunt! It will mean so much to her! Phyllis Lattimer said you were just the person we needed. It would be an act of great kindness. You will, won't you?"

I don't remember much about the chemistry I learned in school. I do remember there were certain things they called precipitates that miraculously sent all solids to the bottom of the test tube, leaving nothing but clear water on top. And that's precisely what Phyllis Lattimer's name thrown into the emotional cauldron did for me. Only it wasn't clear water on the top. It was pure concentrated venom. I glanced through the wide doors at Jennifer Reid's slim staunch little figure and the proud dark curly head being glad about somebody else's husband, knowing as she must that her mother was getting in a few well-timed licks while her back was turned. I knew instantly that the solids precipitated in the bottom of the cauldron were on her side, and that if Phyllis Lattimer was going to be circumvented I was the person who could do it. I knew too that whether Jennifer liked it or not, I had to go to Strawberry Hill. I turned to Mrs. Reid.

"Of course, if you really would like me to . . . I'd be delighted."

Mrs. Reid smiled charmingly, not with relief at all, which surprised me somehow, but with the poised satisfaction of a woman who'd finally got her way. She held out her gloved hand.

"Thank you, my dear. Jennifer will come for you at half past four. It's been *such* a pleasure!"

I looked up. Jennifer had come back into the side doorway. Her face was pale, her blue eyes were liquid black. She wasn't far from tears, but they were tears of anger and defeat. She shook hands with me briefly and followed her mother out. I stepped back to the long open French windows and watched them from behind the gold curtains crossing the empty piazza. I heard Jennifer's voice, low and hot, say, "Mother! You don't know what you've done!" and saw her mother raise her brows without answering audibly. In an-

24

other moment she'd stopped to talk to an old colored woman with a basket of jonquils and white narcissi (butter and eggs, they call them) balanced gracefully on her turbaned head, an old pipe in her mouth.

I picked up the four cards Mrs. Reid had left on the table. The first two were:

MISS CAROLINE COLLETON REID
MISS JENNIFER CAROLINE REID

Each of them had "Strawberry Hill Plantation" engraved on the lower left-hand corner. The other two were:

MRS. ATWELL COLLETON REID
MR. ATWELL COLLETON REID

Each of them had "24 Landgrave Street" in its corner.

I put them in my pocket. If the number of Reids was confusing, it was no more confusing, I thought, than the names like it in Charleston. One thing they did was to indicate the clear and definite cleavage of the two households— mother and son, great-aunt and daughter. I hadn't, somehow, realized they were so clearly divided before.

I heard the fountain playing in the pool, knew thereby that lunch was being served, and strolled out. I had the uneasy conviction that Phyllis Lattimer was being less than frank with me . . . and that she was playing with a stacked deck. Just why I hadn't thought of that before I don't know. Life had stacked the cards for Phyllis the day her grandfather discovered it was more profitable to make and sell guns at home than go and be killed by them on the battlefield.

Nevertheless, I waited for her to call me up, and was a little uneasy when she didn't. I was more than uneasy when I went out after lunch to have a look about the town and passed her maroon mustard-yellow-leather upholstered sports car standing in front of Mrs. Atwell Reid's white house in Landgrave Street.

I didn't really expect Jennifer would come for me, but I had a pretty good idea that if she didn't Phyllis Latimer would, and that I would be got out to Strawberry Hill some way or other. But Jennifer came. Promptly at four-thirty she drove up in a coupé that looked even dingier and sandier and older than it was in the line of elaborate limousines with Northern licenses and uniformed chauffeurs in front of the Villa. I came down the stairs between the white columns with their painted urns full of spring flowers to meet her. She gave me a perfunctory smile with her facial muscles. Her eyes were wary and resentful, and her face a little pale

25

still. She just missed being rude, but it was taking an effort, even with three hundred years of Charleston breeding behind her to make being gracious as automatic as breathing.

I got in her car. Her hand on the gear shift and her foot on the clutch were sure and smooth. That somehow always makes me feel better about people, and I didn't particularly mind that she never bothered about the stop signs at intersections as we went along the South Battery and turned into Ashley Street. We passed Colonial Lake—Rutledge Pond, the natives call it—and went through the blinking yellow light by the Art Gallery without either of us saying a word. As we turned at Cannon Street and took the short cut across the marsh through the line of palmettos to the Ashley River Bridge she said,

"I don't want my aunt to sell Strawberry Hill."

She said it as if she'd been trying to get it out, but also as if it had popped out suddenly when she hadn't expected it to.

"I'm not trying to buy Strawberry Hill," I said evenly.

"I know you're not," she retorted. "Phyllis Lattimer is— and you're the opening wedge."

At the end of the palmetto row she slowed down, glanced around at the main road and shot across in front of an oncoming oil truck onto the bridge. The slanting afternoon sun painted the marsh grass along the blue river toward the Citadel mauve and yellow and brown.

"You don't think she's offering to publish Aunt Caroline's memoirs for nothing, do you?"

I've learned over a period of years that if you can't think of anything to say, it's best to say nothing. In this instance that's what I did.

"I know it means a lot to my aunt. She's been writing them for years. Maybe they ought to be published . . . but it's not fair, it's *just not fair!*"

Just what the connection between selling the plantation and publishing the memoirs was, I didn't know and I didn't care to ask. That the two were connected in Jennifer's mind was enough. The idea that it was the furniture in Strawberry Hill that Phyllis was after apparently hadn't occurred to her.

"Is that why you won't let her in the house?" I asked. "—Phyllis, I mean?"

She turned right on the Ashley River road where the signs on the left point to the road to Folly and on the right to the great gardens along the Ashley.

"That's one reason," she said shortly. "There are plenty of others."

We went along through the sparse sub-suburban dwellings, past the scattered blue-shuttered Negro cabins with their chicken yards and gay pink flowering peach trees, until we came to that lovely stretch of great live oaks with their long

26

smoky festoons of Spanish moss, this side of St. Swithin's Creek.

"Oh, can't you see, Diane Baker!" Jennifer cried, with a sudden almost fierce poignancy. "Can't you see? We've owned Strawberry Hill for three hundred years. It's the land, and it belongs to us, and we belong to it! My family raised indigo and rice on it . . . the people on it were theirs . . . they were using it to make life, not just to spend a few months in the winter playing on it. It's just twelve hundred more acres to shoot over to Phyllis Lattimer—it's everything, everything, I tell you, to me! I won't let them sell it to her!"

I heard myself saying, smugly, "But if it means comfort for your aunt, and your mother . . ."

"Comfort!" she cried hotly. "Is comfort the only thing left in the universe? Did the people who saved it from the Spaniards and built it up and fought three wars to keep it . . . did they go around bleating about comfort? If they had, the Indians would still be shooting wild turkeys with bows and arrows and there wouldn't be any Strawberry Hill!"

There was so much in what she said, and she said it with so much youth and so much passion, that I was ashamed of myself.

"I'd rather die in poverty," she cried, "than sell out year after year, just because we're too supine to work and make the land work when anything will grow on it. Just look at it!"

She waved her hand at the teeming sub-tropical growth on both sides of us, stretching forward and back as far as we could see.

"Other people are doing it. It's just because we're too lazy and too spoiled and unintelligent! It's wrong, I tell you, to waste it. If it were barren and poor, it wouldn't be . . . but it isn't, it's marvellous!"

She stopped abruptly. We'd come to the narrow stone bridge on St. Swithin's Creek that divides the broad tract of land that comprises the two plantations, Darien and Strawberry Hill, on the Ashley in St. Swithin's Parish, before you come to Church Creek and St. Andrew's in St. Andrew's Parish. The whole grant had originally been Darien, but it had been divided, Phyllis had told me once, by Miss Caroline's great-grandfather in 1760 and the smaller plantation given to a widowed daughter who called it Strawberry Hill. It had descended with Darien itself to Miss Caroline's father, who'd left them both to her, his eldest unmarried daughter. As they'd always been in the same family, they'd always kept the single entrance through a fifty-yard double lane of old moss-draped magnolias until it crossed a narrow inlet. It divided then into a wide "V" down two long avenues

27

of live oaks to Darien on the left and Strawberry Hill on the right. We turned in, Jennifer and I, through the old mauve brick pillars, newly painted, with their great carved stone acorn capitals painted fresh clean white, and the elaborate iron gates new shining black, and crossed the bridge.

The avenue to the left was swept sandy-smooth and leafless, its wide grass borders under the moss-hung oaks trimmed and immaculate. A small white shield at its entrance said "DARIEN." The avenue on the right was blocked with a weather-beaten rail gate in the old crumbling brick wall overgrown with yellow jasmine and tangled creeper. I'd seen it many times, of course, from this end, but I'd forgotten about it. And what a wilderness it was—all overhung with moss and flowers so sweet the sense faints picturing them. Was it Shelley who said that? It was true of all this.

Jennifer unlocked the padlock and opened the gate. I drove the car in and stopped while she closed the gate again and came back and took the wheel. Her firm little jaw set. The contrast of Phyllis's avenue into Darien and this one into Strawberry Hill made her struggle to keep it so hopelessly tragic. She said nothing however. It wasn't the traditional Southern lady acting as if the fried fatback were the turkey stuffed with capon stuffed with duck stuffed with doves sort of thing. It was much more human . . . I'd asked for it, and I was getting it, and I could take it and like it.

4

Ahead of us for half a mile stretched an overgrown cavern of live oaks hung with cascades of pale wisteria and thick festoons of grey moss that were more shadow than substance in the low slanting planes of the evening sunlight through the young-leafed branches. Somebody had said the live oak avenues were like cathedral naves. This one wasn't—it was too impeded with magnolias and holly and snowy dogwood and cassina that had seeded themselves among the old trees and stretched up, seeking the sun. But the grey moss and purple wisteria, and the whole glow and loom were very like the clouds of incense from the high altar of Chartres, with the amethystine lights round it making planes as tangible and solid in the darkened aisles as these planes were intangible and ethereal. The broad aisle itself was overgrown with lush green grass, and where the water had settled in the ruts there were tiny iris and white violets. And it was silent . . . so

28

silent you could hear the wind whispering softly in the pine-tops beyond the oaks, like the insistent murmur of long dead voices.

Jennifer put her foot abruptly on the gas. The engine whirred. Half way along the avenue the white tail of a doe flashed, and then another, and another. Still she didn't speak, as we rattled over the bumpy road that was scarcely a road as much as narrow tracks across an overgrown lawn. And then, under the pale mauve canopy of moss and light and wisteria with its arabesque of waxy dogwood, I saw the six slender columns of the portico of Strawberry Hill.

As we came closer the silence came again, so profound that it drowned the cough of the engine and made it impudent and easy to ignore. I glanced back. The avenue closed in, opaque and shadowy as a column of amethyst quartz behind us. Jennifer stopped the car in a drive that would have been scarcely definable if it hadn't been for the marble pedestal that marked the center of it. On the pedestal were two exquisitely lovely marble feet, the heel of one raised just a little, as if a nymph had poised a moment, and two fragile ankles, and nothing else.

Jennifer's eyes followed mine.

"The war," she said briefly. "But they didn't burn the house, or loot it either."

She looked at me with a little frown, as if she were remembering something. But it passed quickly and she got out of the car.

I stood for a moment on my side, looking up at the slender columns of the portico. This house was dead. The four deep windows on either side of the broad front door were barred and shuttered. The door itself looked as if it had never opened. The steps up to it had rotted at the ends, the graceful wrought-iron balcony over it sagged a little. The narrow palladian window with a bunch of strawberries carved in the key over the center arch was shuttered on the inside. The three broad windows upstairs on either side of it were shuttered too.

For a moment we both stood there. My heart throbbed against my ribs. It was so desolate and blind and tragic, someway, with an eerie silence stretching from the tomb of years. I looked at Jennifer. She was looking me squarely in the eyes, and yet way past my eyes, deep inside me—tragic herself, but very young, and with the kind of defences that only the young trust in.

I heard my voice, quite loud because there were no other sounds, say,

"I think I'd rather go back, Jennifer."

I don't know now why I said it. I'm sure I never intended to. It was almost as if I already knew the secret of that old blind house . . . the secret this child had tried so desperately to guard.

She shook her head.

"I didn't want you to come, but you're here now. You can't go back . . . not now. Shall we go in?"

Her voice was perfectly calm, but I saw the corners of her mouth tremble. I followed her up the steps. She unlocked the broad dingy-white door with a big iron key and pushed it open. It was cold inside, cold and damp. I stepped over the threshold. My foot on the side cypress boards, scrubbed clean but not polished, sounded loud and hollow. Jennifer closed the door quickly behind her and drew the bolt. The hall was wide, and even darker than I'd known it would be. The only light was from another palladian window where the delicate sweeping staircase made a balcony across the other end. The door under the stair balcony was closed, an iron bar fastened securely across it. In the dim light from the upstairs window I could see the bold simple cornice and panelling—dingy and split in some places but very fine—and four handsome doors, two on either side with a carved urn of strawberry leaves and blossoms and fruit between the curling rosettes of their broken pediments. It was a fine interior, not as overelaborated as many Low Country houses but bold and masculine . . . not of the diddling Adam that was so popular in Carolina. I glanced quickly at the furniture in it, and saw what Phyllis meant. It was quite perfect. The Chippendale console table with reeded legs, the tarnished girandole above it, the Sheffield urn full of camellias in the center . . . and one of the set of ribband backed Chippendale chairs beside it. I didn't blame Phyllis for wanting it or even for trying to get it, actually. Or the Sheraton sofa against the opposite wall with the relief of rice sheaves carved on the back. Or the Sully portrait hanging over it. Or the Aubusson rug with its trailing border of strawberries that must, I realized, have been woven especially for that space.

Jennifer pulled off her hat and tossed it with her car keys on a Chippendale chair beside the table. "If you'll sit down a moment, I'll see if my aunt is awake," she said evenly. I walked across the hall and sat down in the sofa, something vaguely disturbing nagging in the back of my mind. Jennifer went quickly along the hall, and ran lightly up the stairs. I heard the rapid tattoo of her heels deaden and disappear.

I glanced at the closed doors into the shuttered rooms, and got up. I don't think I intended actually opening the one nearest me, though I know only too well how thin the veneer of civilization is on a professional decorator. There was something else in my mind . . . or possibly, I told myself, it was only to get off the horsehair sofa, that always makes me appreciate the fortitude of the people who wore shirts made of it for their sins, that I got up. Then I sat down, abruptly—for my own sins or Phyllis Lattimer's, I'm not quite sure which.

A door under the stairs was opening, so quietly and so slowly, and without visible human agency, that a chilly prickle crept up and down my spine in spite of all sense or reason. Although perhaps not . . . I'm not nearly so sure now as I would once have been that reality is something one can always be so positive about. But that was later, and now, sitting there perfectly motionless, watching that slowly opening door, I saw, so dimly that it really did disturb me, a trembling black claw pressed against the dark cypress panel, and heard a dull thump-thump.

A tiny bent creature, as black as ebony, with a clean white kerchief around her head, crept out into the hall. She had a flat reed basket, the kind they send camellias in, in one hand and in the other a knotty stick to steady her crumbling joints. She didn't see me sitting there in the dim half-light. She tottered slowly across the hall and stopped, supporting herself against the carved frame of the door nearest the entrance. I waited, a sharp almost breathless excitement constricting my throat. I hadn't realized till then how overpoweringly stimulated my even normally pretty offensive amount of curiosity had been by Phyllis Lattimer and Mrs. Atwell Reid and Jennifer . . . and by the three pieces of old furniture there in the hall.

The old Negress moved her stick to the hand that held the basket, fumbled about in the folds of her skirt, and brought out a key. She put it in the lock and turned it, and turned the small polished brass knob. Then she switched the stick back to her right hand and pushed the door open.

I half rose from my seat, stopped and sat down again, not abruptly but very slowly.

Then I knew. But I'd known it already. It had nagged at the back of my mind the instant I'd walked across the threshold of Strawberry Hill, and again when Jennifer had crossed the hall to go up the stairs. Still I stared through the handsome carved door frame, with its broken pediment and carved little urn of strawberry leaves and blossoms and flowers, to the fireplace beyond. And I knew the secret of Strawberry Hill. I knew why Jennifer Reid had so desperately resisted my coming . . . and why the doors and windows were bolted and shuttered.

Strawberry Hill was empty. There was no furniture in it. No Chippendale settee with a ribband back, and except for the one, no ribband-back chairs to match. There wasn't even a mantel behind that door, or a cornice, or any of the old carved panelling. Even the woodwork was gone; and the walls and chimney breast were bare and maimed and covered with black cobwebs where the panelling, the cornice, and the mantel had been ripped out—ripped out and sold. There was nothing beyond those doors—nothing but a pile of Irish potatoes on an old cracker sack in the middle of the cypress floor. I sat perfectly still, a sick and dreadful feeling in the pit of my stomach.

The old colored woman bent painfully down and started putting potatoes in her basket tray. I kept thinking, over and over, Jennifer didn't want me to come, and this is why . . . but her mother did want me to come—and why did she? The first was clear. The second was not only not clear; it was profoundly disturbing. Did she know . . . or did she only guess?

Then suddenly I heard Jennifer's quick step sounding and echoing in the empty house. The girl who was saving the treasures of Strawberry Hill for herself was coming back.

5

A perfect panic seized me as I realized that Jennifer Reid must never know I'd seen the maimed walls and mangled chimney breast, and the pile of potatoes on the floor of the empty room . . . not ever in the world. I got up quickly and went to the foot of the stairs as she came down the short flight to the balcony landing, out of sight of the open door and the old colored woman picking up potatoes.

"Shall I come up?" I tried to sound as casual as I could.

"Oh yes, do."

She seemed a little taken aback at my forwardness. I went up the stairs, trying not to hurry.

"You must have frozen, down there," she said, looking at me rather oddly. Whether she thought I'd tried to open one of those elaborate locked doors, and failing, had been about to be caught in the act of peering through a keyhole when I heard her step, I wouldn't know. My—I'm afraid—ill-concealed anxiety to be out of the hall and up the stairs couldn't have been particularly reassuring if she did.

"Oh, isn't it lovely!" I heard myself saying, much too brightly, as I crossed the landing and paused an instant in front of the palladian window to pull myself together. I'd said it was lovely quite automatically, just catching, as I came up, the blue glint of the river in the distance. Now, directly in front of the window and looking out of it, I got a positive shock. Below me was an old garden. I'd expected that. What I hadn't expected was to see a garden walled in on both sides with dark carefully clipped camellia trees and banks of early azaleas blooming against them, or the wide borders of white and magenta stock making a flowery cross of the neat transverse brick paths, with an old sun dial set in the center in a velvet bed of multi-colored pansies . . . or the terraces, broken down a little but still carefully tended, running to the pale green and gold marsh on the river's edge.

It was like coming—in fact it was coming—on a perfect formal landscape in the midst of a tropical wilderness. I think I must have gasped quite audibly. The contrast with the oak avenue, completely run wild, and the mutilated empty room, and all they both implied, was suddenly overwhelming. I was literally staggered.

I turned back to the stairs. Jennifer was waiting calmly. She didn't say any of the things I think I would have rushed to say if I'd been in her shoes. In fact she said nothing at all. She simply turned and went back up the stairs into the hall. I crossed the landing and started up too. Then I turned around. I couldn't help it—I think I still didn't believe my eyes. And I started again. A brown and white English setter bounded through the gate in the wall of dark green pollarded camellias, and behind him, strolling casually, his pipe in his mouth, a stick in his hand, with the air of being completely and intimately at home, was Rusty Lattimer, Phyllis's husband.

I should have been inured to shock by then. Still I looked at Jennifer. She hadn't seen him, I was sure of that. She'd crossed the wide hall and was standing, waiting for me to come on up.

The hall ran the length of the house to the shuttered palladian window with the sagging iron balcony that I'd seen under the portico as we came in. It had the same twilight darkness, in spite of the landing window, that the downstairs hall had, and the same closed doors. Except for that on the right, leading to the room overlooking the gardens, the woodwork on them was quite simple. It was much more elaborate, wide with fluted pilasters with the strawberry motif in the carved capitals. It had double doors of polished cypress with silver knobs, and was obviously the entrance to an upstairs drawing room. The hall itself was furnished sparsely. A mahogany highboy stood between the closed doors to the right, and an old Spanish needlepoint chair beside the drawing room door.

Jennifer turned, her hands resting a moment on the silver knobs.

"You know, don't you, that Aunt Caroline is very old, and almost blind . . . and quite deaf?"

33

I nodded. She opened the door, and I followed her into the drawing room. I think I'd known what to expect, though if it hadn't been for that garden I'm not sure I should have. At that, I don't think I expected anything as fine as I got. It was a large panelled room with elaborate cornices, and in the center of the side wall a handsome fireplace with a gorgeously carved overmantel, with the broken pediment and urn of strawberries again. In the overmantel was a painting, dingy with years, of a hill with Grecian ruins on it. A wood fire was burning behind a set of polished brass andirons, and an exquisite Chippendale horse fire screen stood in front of it. The rest of the ornate and handsome old room was perfect of its kind, and I don't know a kind that's lovelier. From the Crown Derby vases and French enamelled clock on the mantel to the old gilt Chippendale mirror, blind with age, above the marble bracket table on the opposite wall, from the worn Aubusson carpet on the floor to the pair of waxed and polished Sheraton card tables on either side of the center window of the river front, they were what dealers like to call "museum pieces." The tall mahogany secretary on one side of the mantel and the rosewood press on the other were museum pieces too . . . but the most perfect one of all was the fragile dresden china figure of the little old lady sitting erect in a faded rose velvet wing chair beside the fire, facing the long windows overlooking the garden and the river.

Her face, as delicate and transparent as a bit of new eggshell, was turned toward me, her clouded eyes open, a smile on her frail lips.

"This is Diane Baker, Aunt Caroline," Jennifer said.

Miss Caroline raised her soft hand. I took it. Its delicate bones under the thin bloodless skin as soft as down pressed my hand gently.

"You seem disturbed, my dear."

There's no use telling any one who knows from the touch of your hand that you're disturbed that you're not, when you definitely are, so I didn't attempt to deny it.

"It's so lovely out here, after the frozen North and the tourists in Charleston," I said, feeling a little guilty. I don't know why one tourist always feels free to deny other tourists the right to exist, but they do, and anyway I was only taking a leaf from Phyllis Lattimer's book.

"My niece wants me to go back to town to live," Miss Caroline said. "But I prefer it out here, myself."

I looked again at the small white head with its little lace cap and the black faille gown with soft filmy white ruching in the throat and at the wrists. There must, I knew, be a body in it somewhere, but it was so frail that the silk seemed to support it in the velvet cushions of the big chair, rather than it to support the silk.

34

"I haven't been at the No'th since the season of 1881," Miss Caroline said. "Your grandmother's parents gave a number of entertainments for me then."

"Perhaps you'll come again," I said.

"No, I think not," Miss Caroline said. "Jennifer and I are too busy managing the plantation. There's always a great deal to do, and I'm getting older, of course. But we find plenty to do."

"Aunt Caroline spends most of her time writing," Jennifer said. She looked at me, putting it squarely up to me. If she'd seen Rusty Lattimer outside, I might have thought that that was why she wanted this interview to get to its point and be over with, but she hadn't, I knew quite well.

"Just a few of the recollections of my life in the Low Country," Miss Caroline said. "For Jennifer's children. The world has changed so much. I should like them to know some day that there was another life, and that it had its beauty and satisfaction as well as its travail."

I looked at Jennifer. She had turned away quickly and was staring down into the crackling pine fire. It seemed to me my cue was obvious, so I said,

"Have you thought of having your memoirs published, Miss Caroline?"

"My niece Mrs. Atwell Reid tells me that Mrs. Lattimer —she married Russell Lattimer's son; his mother was a Roberts, her sister married one of our cousin Colleton's first cousins on his mother's side—Mrs. Lattimer says you have a brother who's in the publishing field."

"My brother John," I said.

"When I was a girl I wrote a number of pieces for the paper," Miss Caroline said. "They were anonymous, of course. My father wouldn't have approved of my appearing in print. But they were accepted, and I've always written a little from time to time. Of course my eyes aren't as good as they were, and my limbs are quite useless. To be entirely truthful, I haven't been out of this room, except to cross the hall to retire in the evening, for over ten years."

I glanced at Jennifer's back, stiff as a frozen willow wand in front of the fire. It was all becoming so clear . . . the room we were in, the furnished hall, the beautiful garden out of the windows. It was like a movie set, only real where the eye of the camera caught it . . . except that Miss Caroline's half-blind eyes were the camera, and she was the star too, and the audience for whom this elaborate façade set in the midst of desolating emptiness was so meticulously maintained. And who had done it, I wondered? It wasn't Jennifer. She wouldn't have been old enough, even if this had happened as little as five years before, to have any part in it. Col-

35

leton would have been only twenty-three, and anyway it seemed to me hardly the kind of thing a young man would ever have thought of. It must have been their mother . . . it just couldn't have been anybody else. But why? And how was it that the whole load of maintaining the pathetic travesty had fallen on Jennifer's shoulders?

She'd turned around, her face very pale. It isn't fair, I thought; she oughtn't to have to suffer this way. For she was suffering. Every taut line of her slim body and the blinding tears she was trying desperately to fight back showed it.

My mind flashed back to the scene we'd had in the Villa drawing room that morning. Why had her mother been so insistent that I come?

"My niece Mrs. Atwell Reid thinks that if I arrange to publish my papers, it will be necessary for me to return to town," Miss Caroline said. "She feels of course that I should have a competent overseer here, because it's a considerable responsibility for Jennifer——"

"It isn't at all, Aunt Caroline—I love it!" Jennifer cried quickly. "I don't want to go back to town."

Her eyes pleading with me not to destroy this grand illusion were more poignantly moving than I could bear.

"I don't see at all why you'd have to go back," I said. "I understood Mrs. Lattimer would undertake to have a . . ." I hesitated. I didn't like to say "ghost"; the whole place was already crowded with them. ". . . An amanuensis." That, I knew, was a word Miss Caroline would understand. "To arrange your material for you."

I glanced at Jennifer. Her eyes had frozen, the hot color surged into her cheeks almost as if I had slapped her face.

"I mean, if Mrs. Lattimer wants to arrange all this as she says she does, there's no reason why the papers shouldn't be taken to her. She could have someone go over them, and——"

And I stopped abruptly. I was looking at Jennifer. She was standing, her head raised, motionless, like a bird dog pointing a covey of quail. The edges of her fine nostrils quivered with alarm. I listened. Then I heard it too: It was a motor car; and for an instant that in itself didn't seem particularly strange to me . . . not a millionth part as strange as the extraordinary way Jennifer was acting. Not until she whispered in a half-frozen little voice: "I didn't lock the gate."

Then the whole business of the barricaded padlocked road, the locked and barred doors, the shuttered windows, rushed into my mind as she turned and flew out of the room, her frantic steps echoing through the desolated house.

Miss Caroline's bewildered half-blind eyes turned to me. "Whatever possesses Jennifer?" she asked.

"A devil of somebody else's making," I thought to myself. Aloud I said, "I think some one's at the door."

"That would be very pleasant," Miss Caroline said. "We're a considerable distance from town, and very few of my old friends have motors, and no one has horses these days."

She felt for the gold-headed stick leaning against her chair and made a move to rise.

"May I get something for you?" I asked.

She sank back against her cushions.

"Yes, if you will, my dear. In the bottom drawer of the secretary. Here is the key."

She felt in the black beaded bag at her side and handed me a small brass key.

"You'll find a box of papers. If you'll bring them to me."

I went to the secretary and knelt down to unlock the drawer, one ear cocked like a spaniel's at a rabbit hole for a sound from downstairs. I pulled the drawer open. There were two small leather trunks with the initials "A.C.R." and the year 1851 studded on them in brass tack heads. I lifted one of them out and put it on the chair in front of Miss Caroline. She opened it. I saw that it was full of neatly tied packets of closely written paper.

Miss Caroline felt about in it with her fragile bony hands.

"It's not this one, my dear. It's the other one," she said, closing the lid again.

I brought the other one over, and moved the first onto the pie crust table in the center of the room.

Miss Caroline opened the second. It was full of the same sort of packets, but they were tied with string, not ribbon.

"That's it," she said. "I think I'll allow you to take this along with you and hand it to Mrs. Lattimer. If anything can be done with my sketches, I shall be very gratified. I don't feel, as Mrs. Atwell Reid does, that they have any great monetary value, although I would be pleased, of course, if they should have. I'm comfortably off, of course, but I have a great many demands, and Jennifer will eventually need what my father, who was Huguenot, called a dot, one of these days . . ."

And just then I heard steps in the lower hall, and a gay familiar voice, slightly sharpened with triumph, saying,

"I do hope you don't mind awfully my barging in this way, Jennifer, but Diane told me to be sure to come for her promptly at half past five.—My dear, I'm surprised she didn't tell you. I thought that was why you left the gate open. My child! What an enchanting view of your garden—it's lovely! I think it's so smart of you to have it this side of the house!"

6

I drew a deep breath. Phyllis's regard for the truth had always been definitely pagan, but this was just too much.

"I hope to heaven she doesn't see her husband out there," I thought, and I must have thought it aloud, because Miss Caroline said, "I beg your pardon? I don't hear awfully well." I caught myself sharply. "I said, 'Here's Mrs. Lattimer now,' " . . . being a little pagan about the truth myself.

"Oh . . . how pleasant," Miss Caroline said brightly. "She's a Northern woman, isn't she?"

"She certainly is," I replied. I don't think anybody from below the Mason and Dixon's Line would have had quite the unmitigated nerve that Phyllis Lattimer was displaying just then. She didn't even wait for Jennifer to announce her in any way. She came straight in, smiling at me with the most charming effrontery, and ran quickly to the little old lady in the wing chair.

"Miss Caroline! You don't know how much I've looked forward to this. It was so sweet of Jennifer to let me come in. I know people must tire you, and I'll take Diane away immediately . . . but you will let me do something about your memoirs, won't you? It's really a public obligation—you've seen so much and you've lived with so much beauty at a time when the world was really civilized . . ."

Jennifer had followed her into the room and was standing, taut and angry, on the other side of the pie crust table, a pale white line around her red mouth, her eyes the color of molten sapphire. There was another quality in the high pitch of her fine head that I hadn't seen before. It wasn't defeat this time, and nothing that resembled tears. It was contempt, complete and scathing contempt . . . for Phyllis and for me, and the whole tawdry hypocritical business we were concerned in. And we had it coming, both of us. I was only afraid that I who deserved it less would be the only one to be aware of it. But I'd underestimated both Jennifer and Phyllis.

"It's very kind of you, my dear," Miss Caroline was saying, in her frail parchment voice. "I've put out my papers. You may take them with you if you like. I shall be pleased if you and Diane think anything can be done with them. They're there on the table. Diane understands."

Phyllis had got up from her attitude of visiting and adoring magus on the little needlepoint stool at Miss Caroline's feet. Her eyes were darting about the room like agitated minnow.

Normally Phyllis would never waste a second glance at anything in a room unless it was a horse or a man, but she wasn't missing a stick or stitch in this one. And in the swift calculating survey her dark eyes met Jennifer's, and stopped. For an instant as brief as a flash of lightning that strips a tree completely naked they met and held. Phyllis stiffened. Two hot burning spots blazed in her brown high cheeks; her jaw tightened. Then she caught herself and moved her eyes slowly and insolently the rest of the way around the room.

"It's a rather nice room, isn't it?" she said coolly. "You ought to do something about the roof. The panelling'll be ruined."

She said it, however, very quietly. I glanced at Miss Caroline, who said, "What is it, my dear?"

Phyllis turned back, warm and charming again.

"I said what a perfectly lovely room, Miss Caroline."

The old lady smiled. "My father and mother, and their parents too, were married here," she said. "I hope I shall live to see Jennifer married here too."

I looked at Jennifer. There was complete agony in her eyes. She looked down quickly and moved a book on the table, her fingers trembling. It was the second time she'd crumpled under the old lady's solicitous interest in her children and her marriage. I was surprised, and I was disturbed too. And I could have slaughtered Phyllis very happily the next moment . . . and I still don't understand it—or if I do I don't want to admit it, not after what happened the next day.

She sat down on the stool at Miss Caroline's feet and put her brown hand on the old lady's knee.

"You really wouldn't keep her from marrying him just because he's been divorced, would you, Miss Caroline?"

Jennifer's head darted up. She stared at Phyllis, her eyes wide, her lips parted, utterly staggered. And so was I . . . and so, may I say, was Miss Caroline.

"*Divorced?*" she said incredulously. "Who's divorced?"

"Why, Brad," Phyllis laughed. "Don't tell me she hasn't told you all about it! Why, Jennifer!"

"If Jennifer is allowing a divorced man to pay her court, I don't wish to hear anything about it," Miss Caroline said. She spoke with so much ice and so much fire that even Phyllis was stopped for a moment—and a little frightened too, I think.

"Mrs. Lattimer is being funny, Aunt Caroline," Jennifer said quietly. "I hope you won't be disturbed by it. And I think it's time our guests were leaving so you can rest."

Phyllis was on her feet in an instant.

"Oh, Jennifer, I do hope I haven't let the cat out of the bag," she said, loudly enough so that Miss Caroline couldn't possibly not hear it. The old lady made no move or sign.

She sat as stiffly erect as a painted mummy case, her transparent hands folded quietly in her black faille gown.

"Are these the papers?" Phyllis asked brightly.

"No, it's the other one," I said, nodding at the leather box I'd put on the table as she and Jennifer had come up the stairs.

"Oh, good!"

She glanced at it, turned and took the old lady's hand.

"Good-bye, Miss Caroline," she said, so sweetly it wouldn't have seemed possible to me, after what she'd just done, if I hadn't known she had quicksilver instead of blood in her veins.

"Good-bye, my dear. And good-bye, Diane. You must come again. We'll talk about your grandmother. She was a mis'able child but a lovely young woman. You favor her more than your mother did."

I shall never be quite sure how we got out of there and down the stairs. I do know that when we got to the bottom I took Phyllis's arm firmly in mine and kept hold of it till we got to the door that Jennifer had left open, now that there was no use to bar it further that day with the enemy inside the walls. I wouldn't for an instant have put it past her to try to open one of those doors, and finding it locked, to guess the truth—or worse.

Jennifer followed us. At the door I turned and held out my hand. I wanted to say I was sorry for the whole dreadful mess, but I couldn't. I might as well have tried to apologize to a block of marble. She didn't even see my hand.

"Good-bye," she said, and as we went down the rotting stairs I heard the door close and the bolt slip into place.

Phyllis's humming "Everybody Libin' Got to Die" as she got into the open maroon sports car infuriated me beyond reason.

"I wish your nurse had exposed you on a mountain top the day you were born," I said hotly.

She put the little leather trunk on the seat between us and switched on the ignition.

"She did, darling, but a large cat adopted me and brought me up on berries and wild roots."

"It was a rattlesnake, not a cat," I retorted.

"Oh, Diane, you're such a bore. Wasn't I right? Isn't that the most priceless stuff? Did you see the chair in the hall? It's one of the set. I'd have given my head to have got a peek into those downstairs rooms, but you were hanging onto me. I didn't want to make a scene."

"Not after the one you made upstairs, anyway. I shouldn't think you'd have nerve enough ever to look that child in the face again."

"But it's *quite* true, darling. Brad's perfectly mad about her."

"Is she so mad about Brad?"

"Don't be silly. The woman hasn't been born that can resist him when he puts his mind to it. And I'd be delighted . . . if he marries her, and gets this."

She waved her hand around the wilderness.

"It would be grand. I'd have all the fun of having him around without any of the bother. And he'd sell it to me in a jiffy. And I wouldn't have to support him with nothing in return."

"Phyllis, I think you're perfectly horrible!" I said.

"Well, darling—why not? I can't let him starve, can I? And I'm terribly fond of him."

I gave up. There was no use trying to explain ordinary notions to Phyllis.

We were going slowly down the overgrown road under the darkening shadows of the shrouded oaks. Suddenly a dog barked, and out from a couvert bounded the English setter I'd seen in the garden.

Phyllis put her foot on the brake and called to him. "Bill!" She whistled then, and the dog raced madly to the car, barking and wagging his feathered tail full of cockleburrs and trailing strands of moss. He jumped up on the running board, put his feet on the door and licked her face excitedly.

"What are you doing over here?" Phyllis demanded. "Come in." She patted the seat, but Bill, with a final moist salute, was down and off up the avenue toward the house.

Phyllis turned around and watched him. I looked at her. Her face was very curious. The flippant laughter had gone out of it. She was biting her scarlet lower lip slowly and very thoughtfully. Suddenly she looked at me.

"Diane—was Rusty back there?"

She nodded toward the blind shuttered mansion.

I don't know what one ought to do under such circumstances . . . and it doesn't matter now, because I said, "Oh, don't be absurd, Phyllis."

She turned around and sat looking ahead of her a moment, still gnawing thoughtfully at her lip.

"Bill never leaves the yard without Rusty," she said after a little. Then she looked over at me. "You know, that might explain it."

"Explain what, angel?" I asked as lightly as I could. I had a pretty sick feeling in the pit of my stomach. There was a dangerous glint in Phyllis Lattimer's eyes that made the campaign she'd already launched against the girl back there behind the barred and bolted windows of the desolate house seem as mild as milk.

41

"Rusty's renewed passion for the soil," she answered shortly. "It's funny. I never thought of that before."

"He's always been interested in the soil, hasn't he?" I asked.

"Yes, but he got over it," she said slowly. "We were having a perfectly swell time. He was drinking more than he ought, but that didn't matter. Then here last fall it all broke out again. He quit reading *Spur* and the library began to look like a periodical room in the institute of animal husbandry."

She tapped her red fingernails on the ivory wheel. She laughed shortly. "That's pretty funny, if you ask me. Of course, she's always talking about the land, but I thought it was because her roots were in it and she didn't know any better."

She stopped, and then suddenly put her head back and laughed out loud. "Well, I'll be damned," she said. She laughed again. Maybe it was the shadows in the dark moss in the oaks now that the sun had gone down that made it seem as if some one was laughing in a graveyard . . . not very loud, and not because anything was very funny either. In fact it wasn't funny at all—it was terrifying.

"Phyllis!" I cried sharply. *"Don't* be a fool!"

"No, Diane, I'm not being one—I've been one," she said evenly. "—And I'm stopping right now. Let's skip it, shall we?"

"Gladly," I said. "If you're sure you mean what you say."

She started the car again. Her face was still set and pale under the rich tan of her smooth skin.

I didn't want to look at her. My hand on the leather seat happened to touch the little old trunk between us. I glanced down at it, and more to be doing something than for any reason at all I lifted the brass studded lid.

"Golly," I said. "—You got the wrong box!"

She looked down indifferently.

"Don't be naïve, darling. Of course I took the wrong one. How else do you think I expected to get inside that tomb again? That little rat Jennifer won't let me in. And you weren't much help."

I stared at her. "You took the wrong one on purpose?"

"Just a child at heart, aren't you, dear," she said amiably. But only the surface was amiable. The lines were still creased about her eyes, and her lips were tight.

"You know, darling," I said, "you're wasting your time here. With your gift for intrigue you ought to try the international situation."

"The inter-plantational situation is my problem," she retorted. "—And you're coming along."

"No, I'm not," I said instantly. "I'm going back to the peace and quiet of the Villa pool."

"That's what you think—but you're not. You're coming

home with Phyllis. There's an extra toothbrush, and it won't be the first time we've worn each other's clothes. Anyway, it's too far to walk to Charleston, and I'm going to Darien."

That settled it, of course. So when I closed the gate to Strawberry Hill, clicked the padlock shut and got back into the car, we didn't cross the bridge again. We turned into Phyllis's dark beautifully-kept live oak avenue. And we didn't speak again until we came into the white circular drive in front of Darien.

7

The house Phyllis had built on the site of the brick mansion the Federal troops had burned in their rape of Carolina was hardly in the tradition of the Low Country. It was tidewater Virginia, with its central Georgian unit, flanking two-story wings and lower connecting hyphens. Unlike most plantation houses built on high arched foundations for ventilation and protection against the miasmas rising from the damp soil, it hugged the pleasant rise of the ground before its velvet terraces swept down to the marsh-fringed river. Even the familiar pillared portico was different from Low Country porticoes. It was semi-circular, full two stories high, but its fluted Corinthian columns rested on the pink-stone flagged earth and were lost in a riotous girdle of the magenta azaleas that most Charlestonians scorn. Whether it was Low Country or not, it was pretty effective, and even a little breath-taking at the end of the long sable avenue of moss-dripped oaks.

A setter bitch and three awkward puppies playing tag around the old hitching post dashed out to meet us as Phyllis brought the car to a stop a little beyond the entrance. She hadn't said a word since we left the padlocked gate to Strawberry Hill.

She pulled on her brake slowly, still thinking. The puppies yapped at the running board.

"I would much rather go back to the Villa," I said.

"I know you would," she replied blandly. "But you're staying here."

We got out, the puppies and their mother all over us. The big white door opened, the colored butler came out to take the leather box Phyllis had in her arms. I hadn't realized until then that she was in quite the state she was. She gave one of the puppies a sharp kick and said angrily to the servant,

43

"Get these damned dogs out of here. I've told you a hundred times to keep them where they belong."

"Yas, ma'am." The black face in front of the white column was sullen and closed. He dropped his extended hands abruptly, bent down and picked up the surprised little animal. The rest of them bounded to him. He started around the drive.

"Oh, Mark." Phyllis turned, half way across the pink flagged entrance. "Is Mr. Lattimer at home?"

"No'm."

The reply was brief and sullen and unfriendly. He was putting the puppy down in the white sandy drive. Phyllis glanced at him angrily.

"I've told him not——"

"Oh, shut up, darling," I said patiently. "You're just working up a scene. And it's the wrong way to go at it."

She flashed around at me, and stopped abruptly. Coming across the wide lawn out of the mauve and grey spring dusk was Bill the setter, and a little behind him was his master. He wasn't strolling idly, as he'd come into the garden at Strawberry Hill. He was walking rapidly. I don't know what it is about the quality of a mood that reflects in the whole external aspect of a moving figure. It was perfectly obvious, however, that Rusty Lattimer was pretty sore about something. I glanced at his wife. Her face had hardened. We were going to have a scene . . . and what was more, we were going to have it then and there.

"Look, Phyllis," I said. "For heaven's sake, go on in before he gets here, and don't make a bloody fool of yourself."

She looked at me angrily. For an instant we stared at each other like a couple of unfriendly cats. Then she shrugged.

"Okay."

We went inside. I followed Phyllis straight up the stairs—they were lovely hanging stairs she'd copied from the Manigault house in Meeting Street—and into her eggshell and pale jade green bedroom on the river front. She put the box down on the bed. I bent down at her dressing table and picked up her feather puff. In the mirror I saw a familiar figure in a black dress with starched white organdie cap and apron move silently out of the dressing room door. I turned around.

"Hello, Felice," I said.

"Bon jour, madame."

Since Felice, Phyllis's French maid, has never liked me, or any of Phyllis's friends or husbands except possibly Brad, I didn't expect her to be cordial at all. She was thin and shrivelled and acrid as an unripe grape. I've never understood why Phyllis kept her around. Her perfectly noiseless tread, more catlike than human, and those black beady eyes that never missed a move and ears that never missed a word would have had her out of my house in half an hour, but Phyllis had kept her through three husbands and twice as many trips around the globe. She closed the door suddenly behind her.

"How does Felice like plantation life?" I asked—more to get Phyllis's mind off Rusty and Strawberry Hill than anything else, because one look at Felice had answered that question.

"She loathes it," Phyllis said shortly. "She can't get along with the colored servants, and they hate her. She has it in for Rusty worse than she did for Brad at first. Rusty never tries to placate her the way Brad did. If she could put poison in his soup, she'd do it gladly."

"Why?" I asked.

"Oh, everything. Making us stick down here in this hole instead of being on the Riviera.—I don't blame her. I'm fed up too." She flipped up the top of Miss Caroline's leather box, sullen mouthed, picked up a packet of yellowed old letters and yanked at the string.

"Phyllis!" I protested sharply. "Those aren't——"

"Oh, keep your shirt on," she said. "I'm not going to read them." She dropped them back into the box, closed the lid and pushed it away from her. "—You'd better go change." She jerked the jade embroidered bell pull at the head of the bed. Felice came in, as sullen faced as her mistress.

"Put Mrs. Baker in the blue room. Her bags will be here in the morning. Get her some of my things—and don't stand there all day!"

"Yes, madame," Felice answered evenly. At times I've wondered how she stood it. Neither her voice nor her face showed the least surprise or annoyance. She closed the door quietly, and I followed her across the hall to the blue room.

Perhaps, I thought, if Phyllis were left alone she'd settle down. Her wrath was compounded of a lot of things, I knew that. It wasn't just Rusty and his farming or his being at Strawberry Hill. It was the frustration she'd spoken of the day before, and the fact that her assault on Strawberry Hill that afternoon—in spite of the leather trunk and old Miss Caroline—was just another failure for her own ego. She had tried to diminish Jennifer, and Jennifer—though I doubt if she was aware of it—had carried the day. Her pride mightn't clothe her body but it protected her soul . . . and that was more than wealth and arrogance could do for Phyllis.

In a few moments Felice brought me a cyclamen pink lace dress of Phyllis's and some slippers. She laid them across the bed and started back to the door. All of a sudden she stopped and literally turned on me—her sallow face almost saffron, her black eyes like glittering shoe buttons.

"Mrs. Baker." Her voice was like steam hissing out of a radiator. "Make her go away from thees terrible place. I cannot live here. I will die!" She took a quick excited step toward me—her face writhing with hysteria. "They persecute me—*les noires*. They are devils! And thees moss . . ."

She shuddered violently. "It will make me crazy—I cannot stand it!—make her go back to New York, Paris, London . . . anywhere but here! They despise her as *les noires* despise me . . . her husband's sister, their friends, that girl who lives in the rotten house. She is after her husband—he is in love with her. Madame will not listen . . . she is mad! —make her go away, I beg you, Mrs. Baker."

She seized my hand, her hard bitter fingers biting into my skin, her face contorted with a dozen emotions I never want to see again. I tried to draw my hand away, but she held on to it frantically. Suddenly she flung herself onto the floor, her head buried in her arms on the satin chaise longue, weeping hysterically.

"—She promised me that we would go, that I could go at Christmas! Then she would not let me!"

"Why don't you go anyway, Felice?"

She threw her arms out, her face eaten by acid tears.

"I cannot! I have no money. She promised me the money. She will not give it to me!"

She raised her head suddenly, a wild frightened light in her eyes, and scrambled to her feet.

"She is ringing for me. Oh, madame, you will make her go? For her sake—not for me!"

With that she flew out of the door.

"Yes, madame?" I heard her say as she opened the door across the hall. I closed my door and went slowly about the business of dressing. This was not only strange, it was getting stranger by the moment.

I put on Phyllis's cyclamen lace dress and cyclamen moire slippers and sat in the window seat, looking down at the old rice marsh, purple and dull gold in the dying evening. Then after a little a silvery gong sounded through the house, and I got up and went slowly downstairs. I don't think I ever looked forward to going anywhere less. Even what would have been a pleasant prospect of seeing again the best professional job I'd ever done was definitely mouldy. Nevertheless, I went and stood a moment in the door of the enormous room that ran the whole width of the house, the river in back, the oak avenue beyond the portico in front. It was a good room, and it should have been. From the T'ang horses on the carved mantel from the old Courtenay mansion in Edisto to the Allan Ramsay of the Duchess of Shaftesbury and the old French gold-brocaded hangings and eighteenth-century wall paper from the Château d'Olivier in Burgundy, there was nothing in it that wasn't virtually priceless.

Rusty Lattimer, in a wine-colored dinner jacket, was pouring a cocktail from the crystal shaker at the low Chippendale tray in front of the fire. He looked up, his face hard, his blue eyes glinting like angry steel. "Look here," he began, his voice as hard as granite. He stopped abruptly and straightened up. "Oh, I'm sorry. I thought——"

"No, it's just Phyllis's dress," I said. "It's me, really."

"Have a martini," he said shortly. I didn't have the feeling that he was angry at me. It was just that he couldn't switch on and off the way his wife could. He handed me a cool crystal glass and sat down in front of the fire, staring into it.

"Are you having a drink?" I asked, waiting.

"No."

I sipped my martini and just sat there, looking around. Most of the furniture in the room was Queen Anne. I'd spent three months in England getting it together. It had been fun, and the only time in my life that I'd never had to boggle at prices. I looked away from it to the hard-jawed young man who was presumably master of all of it. He was over six feet, I imagine, with crisp strawish-colored hair burned light with the sun, and lighter too because his skin was so brown. When I'd first known him he'd looked much the same, with something awfully healthy and out of doors about him, and tough as a cane brake. Then he'd changed, got sort of flabby from drinking too much at too many parties on too many yachts. That was all gone now. It was only his eyes that had kept on changing. First they'd been a merry twinkling grey. Then during the party era they'd got belligerent and resentful, and now they were hard and dangerous, and there was a determination in them that matched the set clean line of his jaw and that I'd never seen before, and wouldn't someway have suspected he'd have.

He got up and filled my glass again, or half filled it, because at that point Phyllis appeared in the doorway. The thin cold trickle stopped abruptly.

"Hullo, darling!" Phyllis's voice was as gay as a mocking bird in a Judas tree.

Rusty finished filling my glass. "Hullo," he said. He went back and got her a glass.

"Darling, aren't you drinking?" she demanded.

"No."

"I don't know what would happen to civilization if it weren't for women," Phyllis remarked cheerfully, holding out her glass again. Well as I knew her, I couldn't for the life of me have told whether she was putting up an ex-

47

traordinarily convincing front or whether a bath and a white chiffon dinner gown actually had drawn all the wrath from her. But I found out quickly enough . . . in fact, the very next instant.

She went over and curled up in the corner of the pale sand-colored sofa at right angles to the fireplace. "Rusty—guess what.—Diane and I have had the most utterly divine idea! It's simply wonderful!"

Her husband, half way through the process of lighting a cigarette, stopped and looked at her. I may be wrong, but it seemed to me from the expression in his eyes that he was seeing her very differently from what he ever had before.

"We're going to take Uncle Fred's yacht and get a few people and go to South America!" Phyllis said. "Won't it be marvellous? Diane's never been . . . it's really her idea!"

"Yes," I said. "It just came to me . . . all of a sudden."

Phyllis smiled happily. "I'm utterly enchanted!" she cried.

Rusty finished lighting his cigarette and tossed the match in the fire.

"You'll have to count me out," he said curtly. "I can't leave the farm."

"Oh darling, that's all arranged. There's that perfectly wonderful man the Lewises had last year. He's going to look after everything. I was talking to him today. We'd only be gone three weeks."

"I'm sorry, Phyllis," Rusty said. "I'm not going. I'm staying here."

All the charming radiance was wiped off Phyllis as if some one had gone over her with a handful of waste wet with varnish remover. She put her glass down on the table in front of her.

"Why not?" she demanded coolly.

"Because I'm not going to leave the farm."

Phyllis got up. They stood facing each other across the cocktail tray that I'd picked up for thirty shillings at the Caledonia Market, both of them white and angry.

I got up too.

"If you people are going domestic, I think I'll take a walk," I said. I might as well have held my peace—neither of them heard me. But I did take a walk. I went out into the hall and out the front door and stood on the pink flag stones under the high ornate portico, and took a deep breath. I'd only made one error, I thought. The scene between them was not domestic, because that implies somehow that it's remediable. This wasn't. All the rules were off. Two people could never look at each other like that and be at peace together again.

I leaned my head against the cool white wood column and looked down the dim cavern of the avenue. The moonlight

48

touched the moss a silvery grey and glistened on the magnolia leaves.

"It's all so senseless," I thought desperately.

I sat down in a white leather chair by the painted iron table in front of the window. There was no use wishing I'd never come, but I closed my eyes and wished it nevertheless. And then suddenly—whether one of the long windows was open a little or whether their voices had risen so much I'm not sure—I heard Phyllis say with a kind of awful triumph,

"Then you *are* in love with her!"

—And Rusty's reply:

"What if I am—she doesn't know it. She's not in love with me."

There was a long dreadful silence, and Phyllis's voice again.

"Get one thing straight, Rusty. You can't divorce me . . . and I'm not going to divorce you. You'd better understand that right now. You haven't a nickel in the world but what I've given you . . ."

I got up quickly and ran across the pink flag stones and out into the grounds. It was too awful. Suddenly I felt something moist and cool in my hand. Bill the setter was beside me, wagging his plumed tail. Then from the house came the silvery dinner gong again, and I went slowly back.

It was quiet as I stepped into the drawing room. Phyllis was sitting curled up in the corner of the sofa, finishing another cocktail. Rusty was gone.

"Oh, darling—I'm so sorry!" She smiled brightly. "One of Rusty's cows is having a calf or something." She got up. "You'll excuse him, won't you? Let's have something to eat. I expect he'll just munch a bit of hay."

I don't know now whether the awful part of that meal, and the two hours Phyllis and I spent playing Chinese checkers in front of the drawing room fire after it, was the fact that she never once referred to anything that had happened since we left boarding school, or that it was my fear that she would, or that at any moment I half expected Rusty to come barging back into the room and was terrified at what might happen. I only know that at last—does one still say at long last?—when I'd gone upstairs and gone to bed, I closed my eyes with a sense of relief I've seldom experienced.

And moreover I went to sleep. I was dreaming of room after room in a lovely house, and each time I'd open a door the room would be gone, but there were always other rooms ahead of me, and suddenly a door opened in front of me and I was sitting bolt upright in bed, staring at my own door, and it was opening. I blinked, not sure I was really awake, and then I knew I was and that the figure in the soft light from Phyllis's room across the hall was Phyllis herself.

"Diane," she whispered.

I reached out and switched on the light on the bedside table. The clock beside it said half past three. I looked at Phyllis. She was in the white chiffon dress she'd worn at dinner. It was her face that was so startling. It was flushed and excited. Her dark eyes were brighter than I'd ever seen them.

"What on earth is it?" I gasped.

She closed the door, came over and took a pillow from the other bed, and curled up against it at the foot of mine.

"Have you got a cigarette?"

I handed her one out of the tortoise shell box beside me and held out a lighted match for her.

She smoked in silence for a few moments, gazing up at the water color of the cypress swamps over my head. Then she said abruptly,

"—There isn't any furniture in that house, is there?"

I caught my breath.

"How do you know?" I asked.

She didn't answer for a moment. Then she said, "Rusty's known it all the time."

"Did he tell you?"

"No. I haven't seen him. He hasn't come back."

"Then how do you know?"

"I know lots of things," she said. She finished her cigarette and pressed it out in the ash tray I handed her.

"I knew it when I was over there today," she said. "I've been thinking about it, and about things I've never thought about before. The settee the Boylstons have in New York is *that* settee—there weren't ever two of them. And the highboy in Cleveland isn't like the one there . . . it *is* the one."

"Well?" I said.

"It's rather . . . amusing, isn't it?"

"I don't think it is."

"I don't either."

She sat there a long time again.

"I've been thinking about Rusty too. He wants me to get a divorce."

I waited.

"But I'm not going to do it."

"Why not?" I demanded. After all, she'd got two. A third shouldn't be hard.

"Because."

"Are you in love with him?"

"No. I hate him. I never realized it before, but I do. I really do."

"Then I should think you'd be glad to divorce him," I said.

"No, you don't," she replied evenly. "You may think a lot

50

of other things about me, but you don't think that.—Or if you do you're wrong."

She took another cigarette. I leaned down and lighted it.

"I'm going to get even with all these people," she said quietly. "So even that you won't even find a daisy where they've been."

"If there's anything I can do to stop you, let me know, won't you?" I asked.

"Nobody can stop me, darling. I've found my life's work."

She got up and tossed the pillow back on the bed.

"The only thing I can't figure out is, who do they think they're fooling?" she said slowly.

"You," I said. "And me."

"No—they don't give a hang about you or me. It's old Miss Caroline they're fooling, and it's a pretty lousy trick."

"Are you planning to tell her about it?"

"I may. I'm not sure. There are—as you no doubt know —more ways of killing a horse than choking him to death with butter."

She moved back toward the door.

"It's funny," she said, turning around again. "I've been watching the river. And it all came to me . . . all of a sudden. All the things they've said, all of them, and more of the things they haven't said. And that river garden, and the hollow sound when I walked across the hall. Miss Caroline hasn't been out of that room for years, so she'd never know, looking out of those windows."

She gave a short laugh.

"What would happen if she found it out?"

"Oh don't, Phyllis—don't do that! Let her die in peace!"

I was suddenly more upset than I'd been for years.

"You can't, really . . . you can't and mustn't!"

"We'll see, my dear. Good night."

She closed the door. It was just as well I'd been asleep already, because I didn't get any more that night. And the next morning when a colored maid brought my tray I looked as old as King Solomon but I hadn't a shred of wisdom with which to face the day.

After a while Felice came in. Her face was older and sallower, her eyes too bright, but there was nothing else to indicate the emotional turmoil seething inside her. She picked up my things.

"Madame has gone to Charleston," she said. "She said if you wanted to go in you could take the yellow car, and you're to keep it and use it as long as you're here."

That, so far as I was concerned, was the only bright spot on the horizon. I don't think anybody ever got dressed and out as fast as I did after that.

51

8

As I came up in front of the Villa I stopped, so abruptly that I stalled my engine. Across the street, parked against the high curb of the park, I saw Phyllis's maroon car with the mustard leather seats. I started the engine again, parked the car and got out. I went up the broad steps, and as I did Phyllis disengaged herself from a group of people and came smiling radiantly to meet me.

"Darling! Good morning!"

She was as fresh and lovely as the bunch of spring flowers cocked on her blue straw hat, and I thought about as natural. She took my arm.

"You must have thought I was a pig, last night," she said . . . not contritely, just cheerfully. "Well, I've just been to see John Michener. He's a lawyer, and he says what I knew, of course, that they don't have divorces in South Carolina like they don't have leprosy in Chicago. But Reno and Florida divorces are perfectly good . . . under the full faith and credit clause, or something, that means they have to accept other states' laws.

"Then you're going to let——"

"Don't be silly, darling. What's a husband more or less to me?"

I was relieved, but not too relieved. That Phyllis could forget easily I knew. I also knew that nobody on earth could say one thing and mean the opposite more convincingly or more cheerfully.

"Anyway, I'm having a party—a farewell party—tonight, and you're coming. Then I'm going to Philadelphia with you tomorrow, and take Felice. She'll certainly be glad."

She smiled brightly at me. "Okay?"

"Okay," I said. But I still wasn't convinced.

It seems to me now that that day was the longest I've ever spent. It was like being on a teeter-totter with Doctor Jekyll and Mr. Hyde on the opposite end. One moment I'd be up, convinced that the last Phyllis, debonair and essentially a pretty good sport, was after all the real one, and that everything was going to be all right. Then I'd go down with a sharp thud . . . knowing she hadn't suffered any such sea change from the early hours when she'd sat on the foot of my bed, and that nothing was all right. By six o'clock that evening I couldn't stick it another moment. I got dressed and got in

Phyllis's yellow car and went out to Darien. Just what I thought I could do, I don't know. The party wasn't till eight. Perhaps I thought that within that hour or so I could pound some reason into her dark wilful head. I was a little relieved therefore when she met me at the door as gay and charming as she'd been that morning.

"You're worried sick, aren't you, darling," she laughed, pecking my cheek lightly. "Don't be. All I needed was a little shut-eye. I'm a changed woman—really."

And when Rusty appeared I believed it. Not that he'd done a volte-face. He hadn't. He was still stiff and hard-jawed and his eyes hadn't changed much, but he was there acting as host and at least being civil. If his attitude toward his wife was . . . well, say detached, it had the distinct improvement of not being as coldly murderous as it had been the night before. There was even a kind of dumb gratitude in the way he let her direct him putting whisky and soda out on the bar in the gun room. And she treated him with a kind of affectionate mockery of a mother who'd given an obstinate child his heart's desire. And when at half past seven the three of us went out on the terrace overlooking the river and had a martini together, sitting on the old joggling board, me in the middle, my fears and forebodings folded their black little tents and quietly stole away.

It was only when the guests began to arrive, the headlights of their cars stretching up the dark avenue of shrouded oaks like long exploring fingers of light, that they started stealing back again.

Colleton Reid and his mother and Anne Lattimer came first. Two couples from the Navy Yard came, and after a little Brad Porter arrived alone, and then John Michener, the lawyer Phyllis had seen that morning, came. He was alone too. Various other people appeared, some of whom I knew and some I didn't. One palefaced little man with eyes like a hawk's and a thin pointed nose came, wearing a normal dinner coat and collar but a slightly flamboyant black bow tie, the sort artists used to wear. I still don't know why he bothered me the way he did. I know I had the crazy notion at one moment that I was the only person who could see him. Nobody seemed to pay any attention to him. I never saw him eat or drink anything. But when I asked a man who he was he said, "Oh, that's Doctor John. Nobody ever invites him anywhere, but he always comes. It couldn't be Charleston without him. He and old Miss Caroline were engaged once."

"My Lord," I said. "How old is he?"

"That was the trouble. He's only seventy. He was twenty then, but she was thirty. People didn't approve. He's quite well off too, but his blood was red, not blue."

Just then Phyllis's voice rose above the well-bred babble. "Anybody want another cocktail?"

She held up the shaker, looking around. Suddenly her eyes widened. "But look! Where's Jennifer?—Mrs. Reid, isn't Jennifer coming?"

No one would have believed she hadn't just discovered that Jennifer was missing.

Mrs. Atwell Reid, talking to a naval officer's wife at the door of the gun room, looked up. I saw her glance quietly at Colleton.

"My aunt isn't awfully well today," she said. "She didn't feel she could leave her."

"Let me go after her." It was Brad who pushed forward. "It's not a party without Jennifer." Brad, I decided, had already been to several parties that day. His face was flushed and he couldn't ordinarily have helped seeing the chair in front of him.

"I think Rusty ought to go after her," Phyllis said brightly. "He knows a short cut."

Rusty's face hardened. He turned around.

"Sure, I'll go if you think it'll do any good," he said, with admirable self control. I think he could have strangled Phyllis just then.

"It's no use, old man," Colleton said shortly. "I tried to get her to leave Rachel in charge, but she wouldn't."

"Then why don't we have some food?" Phyllis said. "It's in the dining room, and there's Scotch and everything else in the gun room."

I think it was with considerable relief—for some of us, at any rate—that we flocked through the doors across the hall to the dining room. And the food was excellent . . . juicy Bull's Bay oysters swaddled in Virginia ham, sweet potatoes soufflé in orange cups with thin chewy slices of glazed apples on top, and green asparagus from Darien's garden. But that wasn't all. On the plates and on a large silver platter at each end of the table were enormous green mounds of plain boiled cabbage, topped with transparent strips of fatback. My heart sank. I looked at Phyllis. All my doubts were gone; it was Mr. Hyde, not Doctor Jekyll, in the saddle. And just then the big booming voice of one of the naval officers brought all of it out into the open.

"Is this some of Rusty's gold-leafed cabbage we've been hearing about?"

I didn't look at Rusty Lattimer. I didn't dare. Above the friendly affectionate laughter that waited for him to acknowledge his parenthood, Phyllis's voice came instead, as light and debonair as the day.

"Isn't it wonderful? It cost a thousand and we could have bought it for nothing half a mile down the road. And . . .

54

oh, Rusty darling, I forgot to tell you—I had it all ploughed up today and put in two thousand young pine trees."

I don't really know what we'd do without friends. They were in the imminent deadly breach in an instant, ignoring the family skeleton that had clattered into our midst, drowning out its bony rattle with such chatter as you've never heard.

Only the little man who had courted Miss Caroline was silent. And he edged through the crowd and picked up a large silver rice spoon and took another large helping of the cabbage. "It's very superior cabbage," he said quietly.

Everybody started violently. It was apparently the first time most of them had ever heard him open his mouth.

"I think it's a pity you ploughed it up. Mrs. Lattimer," he added mildly in the shocked silence.

Two bright spots burned in Phyllis's cheeks. Then the babble rose again to drown that out too.

I moved to the end of the Sheraton sideboard by the library door, and put my plate down, and glanced up.

John Michener the lawyer was standing beside me. Our eyes met. He smiled faintly. I suppose it was that smile, so completely understanding and tolerant, that made me say what I did. It was unpardonable under any circumstances, and I was surprised myself to hear myself saying it.

"Did she see you about getting a divorce today?" I asked abruptly.

"Divorce?" he repeated. And then, in one of those awful silences again, his voice was clear and slow and horribly, horribly audible. "—Death, Mrs. Baker, is the only release from marriage in South Carolina."

"As many people have found out," Phyllis put in brightly. "It's also the release from a great many other things."

"I would like another helping of cabbage," Brad Porter said loudly. "I'm fed up on spinach."

It seems odd now that we got through the rest of supper as pleasantly as we did. I kept my eyes on whatever it was I ate and drank. I didn't want to look at Phyllis and I couldn't bear to look at Rusty. And when it was over and I got into the gun room it was comforting indeed to hear the Navy say confidently that there wasn't going to be any war in Europe and prove it, whether they believed it or not. War on any remote front was a relief from the bitter guerilla skirmish going on at Darien. And so long as the Navy occupied the gun room, it seemed on the whole the safest place to be.

It was almost twelve when the little man with the flowing tie who had courted old Miss Caroline came in. He went to the bar. The colored boy poured him a pretty heady Scotch and moved the syphon toward him.

"I take it neat," he said. And he did—neat and quick—and set down his glass.

"If I could find my hostess, I should like to go home," he said quietly.

"I'll find her," I said.

I got up and went into the empty drawing room. The house was perfectly still. I could hear voices out on the river terrace. I looked out. Anne Lattimer and Colleton were sitting on the joggling board. John Michener was standing talking to a woman beyond the terrace, pointing out over the river. It was as light as day outside . . . as day in a silver cavern. The glistening river, the frosted terraces and banks of pink azaleas, and beyond them the dark oaks dripping silver moss —it was all another world, as peaceful and lovely as a dream.

I looked for Phyllis. She was not out there. I went back through the drawing room, and stopped. Some one was coming down the stairs. There was something so soundless and secret in the muffled tread that I stepped back instinctively, out of sight of the door. The steps crossed the pine floor quickly to the thick rug, and in another instant I heard the front door open and close again . . . so quietly that my heart that had almost stopped burst violently against my ribs.

I ran to the window and put aside the old gold French brocade, and looked out. Some one was running across the lawn toward the fringe of woods by Strawberry Hill. My heart stopped again. My hand holding the fragile silk was moist and cold. The light figure flying in the moonlight was Jennifer Reid. Under her arm was a large object that I knew. I would have known it without seeing its tan color in the moonlight. It was Miss Caroline's leather trunk.

I dropped the curtain slowly into place and stood there a moment, dazed and with an odd sharp dismay picking at my brain. And then, just as I heard voices on the terrace coming closer, saying, "It's late, we *must* be going—where's Phyllis?" I slipped through the door and into the empty hall and upstairs.

Phyllis's door was closed. I knocked on it and waited. There was no answer. I knocked again. Then I opened it and looked in.

Phyllis was lying across her bed. I stared at her, motionless, my breath rattling in my throat. Her head was thrown back, and across her face was a large thick wad of grey and green and black Spanish moss. Her eyes were wide open and horrible with marble terror. Phyllis Lattimer was dead.

On the floor just in front of me was a piece of paper. Like a person moving in a dream I picked it up. I recognized the thin spidery writing that I'd seen in the leather box the day before.

"My dear Mrs. Lattimer," it read. "I gave you the wrong box yesterday. Will you kindly return it by the bearer of this note, who is bringing you the box containing the papers I wish published. Very truly yours, Caroline Colleton Reid."

I looked back at the limp lifeless figure on the bed. "Death is the only release from marriage in South Carolina" kept going through my brain, over and over. I couldn't get it out. I looked back at the note in my trembling hand.

9

Whether the old wives' tale of a drowning man's life flashing before him in an instantaneous kaleidoscope as death closes in is true, I wouldn't know. I do know, however, that with death already in possession of that silent room, every detail of the last three days flashed before me with such vivid clarity and intensity that I might have been actually living it all over again.—My first talk with Phyllis, the interlude in the court-yard at the Dock Street Theatre, Jennifer and her mother's morning call at the Villa Margherita; Strawberry Hill, and the dinner that night at Darien; Phyllis that afternoon at the Villa, and all my seesawing fears, and Felice's hysterical out-burst, and supper . . . and now this.

Every word they'd said came back to me with new and sharpened significance. "I love her but she doesn't know it. She doesn't love me." . . . "I'll never divorce you and you can't divorce me." . . . "I love her, but she doesn't know it" . . . as if any man ever loved a woman without her knowing it long before he did. ". . . I'll get even with them —so even there won't even be a daisy to show where they've been . . ."

And then, like cold drops of water falling: "Death is the only release from marriage in South Carolina . . ."

It was like a defective tap dripping a maddening under-tone through a paralyzing nightmare. But it wasn't a night-mare—it was real. The silence . . . Phyllis Lattimer motion-less on the white quilted satin bed . . . the note in my hand.

It takes so much longer to say it than it did for it all to happen, although it seemed infinitely long, standing there, my feet leaden, the part of my brain that could will me to move numb. Then from below I heard a high-pitched voice saying, "I know it's customary in these days, but I never leave with-out saying goodnight to my hostess and thanking her."

It was Doctor John speaking. Brad's voice, a little thick, cut in.

"Must be damned awkward these days, old chap."

"I expect you'd know, sir," Doctor John replied stiffly.

"All I mean is, she's probably out ploughing Rusty's cows under," Brad answered. "Phyllis is thorough if nothing. And I say, if you're going back with me it's now or never."

"—Oh, go! Please go!" It was almost as if something inside of me was shouting desperately to them to be gone quickly so no one would ever need to know! And then it seemed to me I was suddenly quite rational again. They couldn't go—if they did they'd have to come back. Phyllis Lattimer was dead. She'd been murdered. It couldn't be hid . . . they'd have to know, the whole world would have to know.

I looked across the room. The white telephone on the low table by the chaise longue grew larger and larger until it seemed to me it was all I could see. I ought to call the police. I knew that perfectly. I ought to put the note in my hand back on the floor where I'd found it, cross the room, phone for the police, and then go quietly downstairs and tell them all that Phyllis had been murdered and they must wait till the police came. Then I should tell the police I'd seen Jennifer Reid creep silently out of the house, with the box of papers under her arm that the note was about. That's what I ought to do. I knew it very well . . . and at the same time I knew it was not what I was going to do. I knew I'd not put the note back on the floor, or phone the police, or tell any one ever that I'd seen Jennifer. I'd already crumpled the note into a hard little ball in my hand, for one thing, and I hadn't a pocket or bag to put it in, and the fireplace was not lighted.

Downstairs I knew there was a fire. I clutched the note tightly. In another instant I'd opened the door and stepped back into the hall and closed the door again. It seemed to me—it still seems to me, although I know one can never really tell for sure—that I was perfectly calm as I went down the hanging staircase until I came to the last step, and stood looking at the little group in front of the door.

Then something happened, as if they were a lot of children playing statues. They froze to immobility just where they were. Brad lighting his cigarette. Colleton Reid holding his mother's old velvet wrap. Anne Lattimer, her hand outstretched to Rusty. John Michener undoing the fastener on his leather holder to get out his car key. Rusty saying goodnight. Doctor John saying, "It's a pity about the cabbages——"

They all stopped dead there, staring at me. My knees had suddenly gone to water. I steadied myself against the mahogany stair rail.

"It's . . . Phyllis," I said. "She's dead."

I'd never fainted in my life, but I suppose that's what I

did then. At any rate I felt myself sagging gently against the curling newel post, down to the lowest stair, and all I was conscious of was a pair of dark prominent eyes fixed on me, like burning coals, out of a thin white face above a flowing black tie, and a sudden swirl of movement around and over me, before I lost it all in the dark. The next thing I felt was cool night air on my face, and my hand held tightly in a man's two hands.

I opened my eyes and saw the star-studded sky through the gleaming columns of the portico. It was Brad Porter bending over me then, not Doctor John. It seemed to me I was waking up after a horrible dream, and then it all rushed over me again. It wasn't a dream, and Brad's hands holding mine weren't a dream. I struggled to sit up.

"Take it easy, old gal," Brad said, releasing my hand.

And my hand was empty. The crumpled note I'd clutched in it so tightly was gone.

"Want a drink?" Brad asked.

I shook my head. Then I said, "Yes—get me one."

I could see a glass of water on the white iron table, but I knew it wouldn't occur to Brad to give a lady water, and I had to be alone a moment.

He got up and went into the house. I looked wildly around on the pink stone floor. The little wad of paper might have fallen there unnoticed in the excitement. But it wasn't there. I got up quickly and hurried into the empty hall to the stairs where I'd sunk down. It wasn't there. I started back to the porch and stopped abruptly. Brad had come back to the drawing room door, and was standing, a glass half full of whisky in one hand, a silver jug of water in the other, watching me with sober narrowed eyes and tight lips.

"What's the matter, sister?" he inquired evenly. "—Lost something?"

I felt myself go suddenly dizzy again. This was a Brad Porter I didn't know and had never seen before. I shook my head and got back onto the portico again somehow and sat down on the wicker leather-covered chaise. Brad's steps behind me were slow and rather terrifying. He put the glass and jug on the table and stood there a moment, not looking at me. Then he came over and sat down beside me.

"Diane," he said abruptly. "—How much of this monkey business are you in on?"

I don't know whether it was the deadly evenness of his voice or the way I caught the whites of his eyes in the shadow as they bored into mine that frightened me. Or whether it was just the old intuition functioning on very thin ice. Or why the witches' chant "Fair is foul and foul is fair" popped into my mind . ... or whether it was Brad it applied to. Whatever it was made me a lot more circum-

59

spect than I normally would have been with any one I knew as well as I would have said an hour before I knew Brad. I wasn't so sure now that I knew him at all, or that I'd ever know him really. I said, "Only as much as Phyllis forced me into."

He kept looking at me for a moment. It's strange how terrifying it is to have some one staring at your face that's in the light when theirs is in the dark and you can't see what's in their eyes. Then he turned away and sat hunched forward, his head bent a little. After a moment he said, his voice still deadly even but strained someway, as if it was taking all the control he had to keep it so,

"Listen, Diane. I know Phyllis was a . . . a first-rate bitch, a lot of the time . . . but she's the only woman I ever gave a damn about. Get that straight, will you?—And she felt the same way about me."

He must have felt my surprise, because he added, "She told me so this morning."

Any one who's been brought up with colored nurses knows that you must speak gently of the dead. I couldn't, nevertheless, help thinking that Phyllis had told a lot of people a lot of things—which Brad knew as well as I did. I said, "What else did she tell you, Brad?"

"Nothing," he said shortly. He got up and stood by the table looking down.

"She said she'd chuck Rusty," he said. He picked up the glass he'd brought for me and tossed the whisky down his throat. "I guess I'm going crazy," he said abruptly, and lurched out between the pillars across the drive toward the dark cavern of the moss-hung oaks. The moon sinking below the sable fringe of great trees blotted out the silver light as he went into the shadows and was gone.

I sat there trying not to think—trying, rather, not to think ungently of the dead. It all seemed so bitterly ironic. Phyllis was upstairs; with her, or in her house, were all the people she was going to get so even with that there'd not be a daisy to show where they'd been. And she was dead. Outside were the only two friends she had in the whole Low Country. One of them, a man who loved her, had been married to her and divorced by her, was barging blindly about among the dark trees; the other, myself, was sitting stupidly, with loyalties so mixed. I kept wondering if I could even call myself her friend.

For I knew Phyllis had brought this on herself . . . just how, or by whose hand, I didn't know—but so inexorably that it was in a sense little less than suicide. No human being can trample down other human beings indefinitely without paying up . . . or I hope they can't. Nevertheless, I told myself sharply, because it seemed to me I'd been forgetting it, murder is murder, whoever does it for whatever reason, and no person can commit it without setting up a whole dark pattern of danger and fear.

I got up, and as I did a shadow fell across the pink stone portico through the open door. I hesitated. Mrs. Atwell Reid came out quickly, and stood wildly an instant. Then she staggered, literally, across to the table where Brad had stood, gripped the edge of it with one hand, lifted the silver jug with the other, shaking so the ice rattled violently, poured some water into Brad's glass and drank it. She put the glass down.

"Oh my God!" she moaned desperately. "Oh my God!"

Then she saw me, or rather she stared at me, not sure, I think, whether she was seeing me or imagining me.

"You'd better sit down, Mrs. Reid," I said.

She just stood stupidly, her hands clutching at the table edge.

"This is horrible, Mrs. Baker!" she whispered.

"I know it is," I said.

She moved unsteadily to the chaise wicker chair and sat down, trying to control her trembling body.

"Thank God Jennifer wasn't here tonight," she said quite suddenly. "This is bad enough. That would have been too horrible."

I've wondered since if it would have made any difference in what was still to come if I'd told her then that Jennifer had been there. I'm not sure even now, though I didn't realize then what I do so strongly now, that Mrs. Atwell Reid was a . . . well, a very Southern woman, a curious mixture of strength and weakness. Maybe "Southern" is the wrong word, except that the combination of strength to keep a whole civilization alive and going, and weakness in the face of prejudice and custom, seem someway very Southern indeed. But I didn't tell her, I couldn't have possibly. I said, "Why?"

"Oh, because," she answered, and then, as if that weren't an answer really, she added, "Jennifer is hot-tempered and . . . and prejudiced. She's like all the Colletons. She takes violent likes and dislikes to people. She never could endure Phyllis. They had a furious quarrel this afternoon . . ."

She stopped, pleating and unpleating her chiffon scarf with agitated fingers.

"I thought it was most considerate of Phyllis to ask about her this evening."

"—Or something," I thought. I didn't say it, and just then I became aware of voices in the hall and heard John Michener say, "Where is Mrs. Baker?"

I got up again.

"We'd better go in," I said.

Mrs. Reid nodded. I waited while she took a small feather puff out of her evening bag, and patted her eyes with it and put it back. She got up and took a few steps. Then she stopped.

"I can't go back in there," she said quietly. "I can't face it, I really can't. You go along, my dear. I'll come when I can."

Her voice was calm, but her face was white in the half-light of the porch, and she was trembling again so violently that she had to sit down quickly to steady herself. For a moment I hesitated too. It seemed very odd that she should be so completely unnerved. She reached her cold hand up and touched mine.

"You see, my dear . . . I've been through all this before," she whispered softly. "It's a very terrible ordeal . . . for everybody."

I'm afraid I stood there staring at her. Surely she didn't . . . Then I stopped abruptly. There was no use trying to speculate. I hadn't enough to go on, and what I had was too muddled and too contradictory to make any sense at this point.

"I'll go on in, then," I said, and hurried over to the open door. "If only I had Jennifer's note," I thought. Or if only any one else but Brad had it. For I was sure he did have it—otherwise why the talk about monkey business? It was only what he might do with it that alarmed me. That I couldn't be sure of.

I crossed the hall to the drawing room door, and stopped.

10

Rusty Lattimer was sitting on the sofa in front of the fire, his face carved grey stone, staring into it. Doctor John, John Michener and Colleton Reid were standing a little to one side, talking in low whispers. John Michener caught sight of me first, and it seemed to me silenced the others, or perhaps just his moving out from between them and coming toward me did it.

Colleton glanced at me and away again quickly, with something so like hatred in his dark burning eyes that I was worried and alarmed even. Just then the door from the river terrace opened and Anne Lattimer came slowly into the room. Her face was frozen and white as death. The rouge and lipstick on it stood out related to nothing, like daubs of paint on a plaster of Paris mask. Only her eyes were alive. It seemed to me suddenly that if there can be private and individual hells, there were three in this room now . . . and the two outside and the one I knew was across the fields in the devastated mansion at Strawberry Hill made six altogether, which is rather a lot of hells. And each, I knew, was different . . . each paved with heaven only knew what intentions.

Anne Lattimer's eyes moved from one person to another, then she walked quickly over to the sofa, sat down beside her brother and slipped her arm through his. It was a simple and natural enough thing, I suppose, or should have been. It just happened that it wasn't. It cut the room in two as sharply as if somebody had materialized a wall of ice through the center of it. It was the first time Anne had identified herself with Rusty in any way I could remember. The few times I'd seen her, she'd been identified with the Reids —with Colleton and his mother. At the theatre, all during the evening just finished, even when I looked down the hanging staircase and saw them preparing to leave Darien, before they knew about Phyllis. But now it was Anne and Rusty together, against all comers.

I saw the sharp tension along Colleton Reid's spine as he turned and took a cigarette out of the box on the table near him. He didn't look at Anne again, nor did she—as far as I could see, and I would have seen it because I was interested—look at him again.

John Michener took my elbow and led me to a chair in front of the fire, exactly, I thought, as if he were lawyer for the defense, leading me to the witness stand. There was something comforting about it, however—or there would have been if I hadn't been so aware of the two dark enigmatic eyes of the little doctor on me all the time.

"I've phoned for the sheriff, Mrs. Baker," John Michener said. "They'll be here directly."

I nodded. He turned to Colleton.

"I think you'd better find Brad, Colleton, before they come. And if your mother is able, I think she'd best be present too."

Colleton didn't move for a moment. Then he turned and strode out of the room. The rest of us sat or stood where we were, listening to the Sèvres clock tick impatiently to the T'ang horses on either side of it who'd already lived so many centuries that they were impervious to its warning. After a little Colleton came back. His mother, paler because of the streak of powder across her bloodless cheeks, came with him, clinging protectingly, and at the same time seeking protection, to his arm. She sat down in a corner of the other sofa and turned off the light beside her. She looked tired and very old, sitting there, her eyes shaded with one hand, her

63

feet in tarnished silver slippers crossed under the hem of her blue lace dinner gown. Colleton went back to the fire and stood as he had before.

Then Brad Porter came in. He came slowly. He didn't say anything or seem to look at anybody. He just walked in and sat down, his knees apart, his hands between them pulling into strands a wad of grey moss. It was terrible, someway. None of us seemed to look at it, and yet from the sudden tension in the room I knew I wasn't the only one who'd never look at moss again without seeing Phyllis. And suddenly Anne Lattimer sprang to her feet, snatched it out of his hands and flung it into the fire.

"Brad, you're horrible!" she cried hysterically.

He didn't move or look up at her. He just sat with his hands motionless and empty. The fire sprang up, the moss glowed an instant and died.

"Sit down, Anne," John Michener said gently.

"I'm sorry!" she whispered. "I guess my nerves are shot." She sat down. Rusty Lattimer hadn't moved a muscle.

"I think all our nerves are shot," Mr. Michener said quietly. He looked around the distraught little group. His voice was kindly and old-school, but I didn't for an instant have the idea that he was prepared to dispense any whitewash. The lines in the corners of his mouth were pretty grim.

"I don't think there's any use for any of us to try to disguise the fact that we're seriously involved in a very serious situation," he said. "I know there are people who think murder in some instances is justifiable. I don't belong to that school, because it is a complete negation of the law to which I've devoted the greatest part of my life."

He paused for a moment, and without looking away from the blazing lightwood fire he said, "You'll forgive me for saying I believe there may be justification for one man to shoot another, for reason, or even in the heat of passion."

Nobody looked at Colleton Reid—not even his mother.

"There may even be some justification for killing a woman in the same circumstances. That was not done here. I think it makes our duty in this instance perhaps clearer than it might otherwise have been.—And now that you know my position as a gentleman as well as a friend . . . and perhaps I might add as Phyllis's legal adviser——"

What I think was intended only as an imperceptible pause to make his point perfectly clear became an abrupt stop. Everybody—even Brad—had turned and was looking at him with such varying degrees of surprise and even consternation that it was perfectly astonishing. At least it was to me. After all, John Michener was Charleston's leading lawyer, and Phyllis had been to law, for one thing and another, a good many times in her thirty years. If she had planned to go again, he was certainly the logical man to see.

"May I ask what she consulted you about?"

It was Brad, oddly enough—or perhaps not—who broke in the strained silence.

"I see no reason why you all shouldn't know," John Michener said evenly. "Especially as some of you know already. She came to find out what the status of a Reno or Florida divorce is in South Carolina, and to instruct me to make the necessary arrangements with our correspondent——"

And that's as far as he got. Rusty Lattimer had got to his feet and was staring at him, his jaw working, his face utterly haggard. Then as suddenly he did very much what Brad Porter had done before him: he lurched across the room and out the river terrace door into the night. The rest of us sat perfectly motionless until Brad got up suddenly.

"I need a drink. What about the rest of you?"

He crossed to the gun room and slammed the door shut behind him.

"I still think it was quite unnecessary for her to plough up the cabbages," Doctor John said quietly. He got up and followed Brad.

He was right, of course. If she'd been going to divorce Rusty, ploughing up his farm seemed a completely gratuitous insult. Stopping the money that supported it would, I should have thought, been quite enough. But one couldn't tell about Phyllis, not ever. And in spite of the fact that she'd apparently been speaking the truth that afternoon at the Villa ("What's a husband more or less to me, darling!"), I still didn't believe she hadn't another trick or two in her hand. Not after she'd quarrelled with Jennifer, anyway. It wasn't like her.

I glanced around at the four people left in the room. Mrs. Reid still sat immobile, her face shaded by her hand. Colleton Reid had moved to the front of the room and was standing, the curtains a little apart, looking out down the avenue of oaks. Anne Lattimer sat bolt upright in the middle of the sofa, staring into the fire; John Michener was looking at me.

I got up. I didn't need a drink the way Brad—and apparently Doctor John—did, but I needed some air. The whole atmosphere of the place was getting me down. Phyllis's still face covered with moss kept coming back to me, and with it the stealthy steps on the stairs, and the slim figure of Jennifer Reid running across the moonlit lawn. I started for the door, but John Michener's voice intercepted me halfway across the room.

"Mrs. Baker," he said. I stopped.

"You've seen a good deal of Phyllis the last few days, haven't you?"

65

I nodded.

"Did you know she was planning this . . . this step? A divorce, I mean?"

I nodded again. "Yes, I knew."

"If you see Rusty out there, will you ask him to come back in?" he said quietly. "I hear the police coming."

I hurried out. The cool breeze from the river touched my face like a healing breath of sanity. Silhouetted against the dying silver of the water I saw Rusty's dark figure. On the other side of the house I could hear a car coming closer and closer and stop, and the sound of a door slamming, and another one. Rusty ought to be there, I thought, and I ran down the white sand path.

He was standing, his hands in his dinner jacket pocket, staring out over the river. I grabbed hold of his arm.

"They've come, Rusty. You've got to go back and see them."

He nodded, but he didn't make any move to go. I released my hold of his arm.

"Don't, Rusty! Please don't!" I said . . . although what it was he was not to do I'm not very sure now. He wasn't doing anything but stand there.

I touched his arm again.

"Rusty! Look—you've got to snap out of it. The police are here. They'll be asking for you. You didn't do this, you couldn't have . . . but it's piling up on you. Don't you see? Whatever way you look at it . . . whether you knew she was going to get a divorce or whether you didn't . . . it's just as bad one way as another. And they're all against you!"

I stopped short. I hadn't meant to say that, because I hadn't been conscious before I said it of even so much as thinking it. But the instant I said it, I knew it was so. They were against him . . . Brad, his wife's lawyer John Michener, even the Reids—everybody, in fact, except the queer little old doctor who had wanted to marry Miss Caroline half a century ago. I'd felt it all the time I was in the house. Why or how, I couldn't have said, but I had, all the time Brad sat there pulling at the wad of gray moss that had finally torn Anne Lattimer from her frozen calm. And I couldn't understand it. They hadn't cared anything about Phyllis, and Rusty was one of themselves. He wasn't an outlander, like Phyllis or Brad or me.

"—Don't you see, Rusty—you've got to go back there now and face it."

He looked down at me, shaking his head.

"You don't understand, Diane," he said slowly. "And I can't explain it to you. It's not as simple as you think."

"It's not as simple as *you* think, my lad," flashed across my mind, but I didn't say it. I said, "That may be, Rusty. But it's

66

simpler than it's going to be if anybody gets the idea you're turning tail and running."

He shook his head again.

"Look, Rusty. Didn't you . . . didn't you care anything for her, really? Don't you feel sorry . . . now?"

"I don't know what I feel, Diane," he said very quietly, after a long time. "Yesterday and last night I could have killed her . . . and tonight at dinner. Now I don't know. It's like having your leg cut off. You don't feel anything at first. You will pretty soon, but you don't now. You don't believe it could happen—any of it. What went before, or . . . this."

It may sound heartless as I repeat it, but it wasn't then. It was just a kind of dumb agony in which all that had gone before—and there must have been a lot I didn't know about —still ached worse than the shock that had released him.

"Well, anyway you'd better come in now . . . and don't tell this to anybody else," I said practically.

I took his arm again, and this time he came. It was like leading a horse that had become docile at a moment when you least expected it. We went up the white sand into the penumbra of the house. The moon had gone down. Through my mind crept the somber cadence of the old blind darkey's chant:

> "When the moon goes down in blood . . .
> When the saints come marchin' home."

This moon had gone down . . . in bad blood and in death; and Rusty, though hardly a saint, was marching home into the very thick of it.

I opened the door and went in. He followed me. It was like going into a room at Madame Toussaud's. Mrs. Reid and Colleton and Anne Lattimer were motionless as waxworks there, in precisely the same spots and attitudes they'd been in when I barged out. They looked as if they'd neither moved nor spoken, and I doubt very much if they had. John Michener had gone, however, and through the open door of the gun room I saw that Brad and old Doctor John had gone too. I could hear the tread of feet upstairs and the intermittent drone of voices.

"Mrs. Abbott said for you to come up when you came in, Rusty."

Anne Lattimer spoke without turning her head. Rusty crossed the room silently, and I heard him go up the hanging staircase. It seems to me that usually you can read something from the sound of footsteps, as people approach a difficult job, but I couldn't in Rusty's. They were neither slow nor fast, determined nor faltering. They were like so much else that night . . . completely enigmatic.

67

I sat down beside Anne on the sofa to wait. Then I got up and put a piece of pine wood on the dying fire. Mrs. Reid stirred a little.

"Colleton," she said, "go ask Mr. Abbott if it will be all right for you to take me home. My head is splitting."

Anne Lattimer darted her a swift cat-like glance, and closed into marble again. It seemed to me that years of frustration and resentment against the older woman had suddenly that night boiled to the surface in Anne Lattimer. It was natural enough, heaven knew. It must have been like having a mother-in-law without whatever solace actually being married to her son might be assumed to afford. There was no doubt, certainly, of the gentle proprietorship in Mrs. Reid's attitude toward both of them. It was very different from the almost drawn-swords relationship between Jennifer and her mother.

As Colleton moved across the room I glanced at Mrs. Reid again. She still had her hand to her forehead, shielding her eyes, but I could see them. They were fixed on Anne Lattimer, and strangely appraising, it seemed to me, though she must have had plenty of opportunity in the last twenty-five years to estimate her fully.

At the door Colleton stopped. Then he went out quickly into the hall and closed the door. We could hear the muffled sound of slow heavy feet on the polished stairs, down to the hall, along it to the front door. Anne Lattimer's hand gripped mine, her nails biting into my fingers. A motor started up, a car moved away. Phyllis was gone, on her last journey under the shrouded oaks. The sound of the car died in the distance.

Anne's fingers gradually relaxed, leaving mine numb and paralyzed. She closed her eyes and leaned her head back against the sofa. The tears squeezed out from under her long dark lashes and streaked slowly down her cheeks. Mrs. Reid did not move a muscle. Then the door opened. A tall thin man, unshaven, his red necktie a little askew and his thick iron-grey hair a little rumpled, came in with one big hand on the narrow shoulder of old Doctor John. I stared at them. For one perfectly absurd instant I had the horrible conviction that the little man was under arrest. Then it all passed as quickly as it had come, as Mr. Abbott dropped his hand and came over a little in front of the rest of them . . . John Michener, Brad Porter, Rusty and Colleton. They were all so grim that it was a little terrifying.

"This is Mr. Abbott, Mrs. Baker," John Michener said. "He's the head of the County Police.—Mrs. Baker found Mrs. Lattimer."

11

I stood up. As Mr. Abbott and I faced each other, I sensed what I now know—that if I were colored and had stolen a hen I wouldn't want Mr. Abbott looking at me like that. Being white and having stolen no hen, I still didn't like it. He had the frostiest grey eyes I've ever seen, and the shrewdest. His lips made a thin wide line dropping at the corners under a long intelligent nose, the tip of which moved a little disconcertingly when he spoke. He had a long upper lip too, and a tiny brown stain of tobacco juice at one corner of his mouth. I had the feeling, even before he spoke to me, that he had sized me up as shallow, vain, unreliable and a Northerner . . . all of which was no doubt true, but one likes at least to have a chance to disprove it.

"They tell me you're an old friend of Miz' Latimer," he said.

I nodded. So did he.

"What time would be it you found her?"

"It was a little after twelve," I said. (I don't know why he frightened me the way he did.)

He looked at his watch, and glanced for corroboration at the Sèvres clock on the mantel. It was twenty minutes to two.

"How did you happen to go upstairs just at that time, Mrs. Baker?"

"The guests were getting ready to leave and wanted to say good-bye to the hostess," I answered, "and she wasn't around anywhere. I offered to go find her. I looked out on the terrace and she wasn't there."

(I must be careful, I thought steadily . . . and he knew that was what I was thinking. I could see it in the hooded look that came into his eyes, fixed on mine.)

"I thought she might be upstairs, so I went up."

"You didn't know she was up there?"

"No."

"You didn't, for instance, see anybody . . . coming down, say, or anything that made you think she was up there?"

"No," I said. (Why should I lie so baldly for a child I scarcely knew when a friend I'd known all my life had been murdered, cold-bloodedly and quietly while the house was full of guests?)

69

Mr. Abbott was looking at me. Something almost fatherly—and infinitely terrifying—had come into his eyes and his voice.

"You're sure about that, Mrs. Baker?"

My heart sank. Did he know I'd seen Jennifer? Had somebody seen her and me?—One of the servants . . . or Brad? I tried desperately to remember where Brad had been. Colleton and Mr. Michener and Anne and Mrs. Reid had been on the terrace. Doctor John in the gun room. Rusty I hadn't seen, nor Brad. No one else could have told him, so he might only be guessing.

I shook my head.

It seemed natural enough that she might have gone upstairs to powder her nose— And then I thought of Felice the French maid, and my heart sank a notch lower. I'd never realized how blind one can be in the stress of the moment. A dozen people, of course, might have been watching me watch Jennifer and I'd never have known it. But I couldn't go back now.

"As I understand it from Doctor John here," Mr. Abbott said, "you left the gun room to find Mrs. Lattimer. He waited a while, but you didn't come back, and a lot of people left while you were gone."

I looked at Doctor John. His bright dark eyes were fixed steadily on me. I didn't know what to say. Actually I had no notion, and I haven't to this day, of how long I was upstairs, holding onto the door, utterly stupefied, staring at Phyllis, or how long I stood with old Miss Caroline's note in my frozen hand.

"I don't know how long I was gone," I said weakly.

Rusty Lattimer's voice, quiet and firm, was like a benediction: "You're not suggesting Mrs. Baker murdered my wife, are you, Abbott?"

"I'm not suggesting anything, Rusty. I'm just trying to get down to facts here. And it looks to me like Miz' Baker ain't telling all she knows."

"I think Mrs. Baker is pretty unstrung now anyway," John Michener said gently. "In fact, I think, if I were you, I'd let all the ladies go home, and see them in the morning. This has been a little hard on them."

He didn't look at either Mrs. Reid or Anne Lattimer. Both of them were considerably more unstrung, as my cook used to call it, than I was. Mr. Abbott knew it too. I suspect that's why he was badgering me. I obviously should have been more unsprung than I was.

"I don't want to be too hard on the ladies," he said. "But there's a few things I'd like to get straight tonight."

He turned away from me. "One is the time. Mrs. Baker says it was around twelve when she found Mrs. Lattimer. She was

70

dead at that time.—What was the last time anybody saw her alive?"

He looked back at me.

"I didn't see her after I left the dining room," I said. "That was about ten. I was in the gun room with several people from then until Doctor John came in, about midnight."

"And you, Doctor?"

"I saw her through that door."

The litle man nodded toward the river terrace.

"She was humming a tune. She said, 'I hope somebody's taking care of you, Doctor—it was sweet of you to come out.' She then went through that door."

As he nodded toward the hall, I saw for the first time that Felice, Phyllis's French maid, was there, in an 'old pink chenille bathrobe, crouching down in her chair, her pointed face saffron-yellow under black hair pulled back tightly from her forehead. I don't know what it was about her that reminded me of a cat that waited, claws bared, to spring. Because there was something more about it, as if the cat had decided not to spring but to wait—just a little for a better moment. It must have been her eyes. They were bright and beady still, but the snapping restlessness in them had frozen to an almost uncannily guarded intelligence.

A sharp alarm stabbed my brain. She'd seen Jennifer, I knew. That was why she was waiting. I saw it in the quick hard glance she shot at Rusty before she lowered her eyes to keep from meeting any one's. Her hands moved, tighter together, in her lap.

"She went out the front door," Doctor John went on. "I didn't see her again. That was five minutes to eleven. I know that because I like to go home by eleven."

Mr. Abbott looked at Rusty.

"I didn't see her after we left the dining room," Rusty said shortly. "About ten, I guess."

"—Mr. Michener?"

John Michener nodded. "I saw her—alive and happy—about a quarter past eleven," he said. "She was out on the front porch. I walked around the wing here"—he indicated the gun room—"to look at the avenue in the moonlight. She was sitting out there by herself. She called to me, and I talked to her about five minutes—about her plans. She was preparing to leave Charleston for a while. I didn't stay long. She seemed to be expecting somebody. I went upstairs and got some of my cigars—they're milder than most—out of my topcoat pocket, came down and joined the young people on the terrace. As I say, she was in the best of spirits at that time."

Mr. Abbott looked at Mrs. Atwell Reid. "—And you, ma'am?"

71

"I don't know," Mrs. Reid said slowly, "—not to speak too certainly—after we left the dining room. Oh yes, I did see her too. She came out on the terrace. We spoke of how pretty the azaleas were in the moonlight. She went around speaking to everybody. Just casually, you know. I didn't see her again."

Mr. Abbott looked at Anne Lattimer.

"I didn't see her after supper. I was out on the terrace all the time."

"—You saw her come in, after she talked to Mrs. Reid?"

"No," Anne said. "I mean yes, of course. I was on the terrace with the others."

Mr. Abbott seemed to have overlooked Bradley Porter. He glanced over Mrs. Reid's snowy-white hair to the door. "And you, mamselle?"

Felice seemed in some curious way to efface herself in the chenille ribs of Phyllis's cast-off dressing gown, seemed practically to disappear in front of our eyes. Yet there was nothing demure or shrinking in it. I thought again of the cat biding its time. She was a sort of Madame de Farge without any knitting. She moistened her lips with her pointed tongue.

"Madame came upstairs," she said quickly. "It was after half-past eleven. I do not know the exact time. She said, 'Felice, go quickly to bed, I am busy.' I said, 'Is Madame Baker staying tonight?' She said, 'Yes, of course, but do not bother about her. Run along, quick now.' She was in a . . . what do you say? . . . big hurry."

It's a fallacy, of course, to think that being French necessarily makes a woman attractive. Mr. Abbott gave me the impression, however, of struggling with his lost youth. If Felice, who was forty and looked a hundred just then, had only thrown in a few simple French words, it might have helped, but she spoke English far better than Mr. Abbott ever would. Still, she was French, and Mr. Abbott had no doubt been A.W.O.L. in Paris in the spring.

"Did you get the idea that Mrs. Lattimer had a . . . an appointment with somebody?" he asked. I didn't know whether he was being French, or delicate, or just plain offensive. Apparently Felice didn't either. Her black eyes blazed up.

"That is not true," she snapped. "She knew I was tired. She wanted me to go to bed. That is the way she was."

"You didn't see anybody come up, either a man or a woman? Because somebody did come, mamselle—somebody either came or was already there.—And he murdered your mistress."

"I saw nobody come, and nobody was there," Felice said tightly. "I was in madame's room, or in the blue room across the hall, all evening."

"You saw Mr. Michener come up, then? He says he did come."

"I saw him come up—and go down again," Felice said. "I saw several gentlemen and ladies come up, get their wraps, and go down again also.—And now, I would like to go to bed. I have put some of madame's things out for you, Madame Baker. Good-night, madame."

And she left. Mr. Abbott watched her go, biting his under lip as her slippered feet padded up the stairs. He looked at Rusty.

"How did that woman get with your wife?"

"She's been with her ten years," Rusty said, in that crisp hard way of his. "She's as faithful and devoted as they come, these days."

"She wouldn't have any old grudge——"

"Not against my wife."

Mr. Abbott looked at him for a long time, a curious glint in his eyes. All the time my mind kept rehearsing that incredible scene of Felice's the first day I came. It was odd that with all the other feline characteristics I'd known in her for a good many years I'd never thought of her as dangerous before. I did now. And Phyllis's "She's such a devil with the other servants" that I must have heard at least once in every town or country they'd lived in picked unpleasantly in the back of my mind. She'd been so patient with Phyllis's histrionics . . . Now that Phyllis was dead, and Felice was alone and uncontrolled in a land she hated, with people she hated, I wasn't sure.

Mr. Abbott didn't seem particularly sure either. He shrugged his lean shoulders as if dismissing the whole matter, and turned to Brad Porter, hunched quietly down in a fireside chair off in a corner of the room, as completely detached as Felice had been.

"I guess that just leaves you, sir."

"I saw her just after Mr. Michener came in the house," Brad said . . . very evenly and with a kind of slow emphasis that made my heart sink suddenly. "—Out on the porch. I talked to her about fifteen minutes, until she came in and went upstairs."

I don't know what there was that made that sound so utterly ominous, but there was something. Mr. Abbott felt it too. I could see him prick up his ears like a bird dog in a stubble field.

If any one can feel wariness, that was what I felt then. The whole room was full of it; it fairly vibrated round every figure there . . . Mr. Abbott probably more than the rest of us.

"If you don't mind," he said slowly, "I'd like to know what the two of you were talking about?"

Brad Porter did not move a muscle, but I had the feeling that he was all tensed, ready to spring. "We were discussing her divorce," he said.

Even though he said it very quietly, it hit the strained silence in the room like a ton of brick.

"Divorce?" Mr. Abbott repeated the word as if he had never heard it mentioned in police society before. "What divorce?"

Nobody looked at Rusty, not even Mr. Abbott; certainly not Brad nor I.

"Perhaps you didn't know Mrs. Lattimer was planning to divorce Lattimer," Brad said coolly . . . and with such monstrous insolence that Rusty Lattimer stiffened and flushed as if he'd been struck full in the face. He stood up and started across the room. John Michener stepped quietly in his path. Brad didn't turn a hair.

"Sit down, Mr. Lattimer," Abbott said. "Maybe we're getting someplace now."

Rusty stood white-lipped, his grey eyes as dangerous as naked steel, his whole body rigid and yet so horribly mobile that it didn't look as if anything could stop him now.

"Sit down, Mr. Lattimer," Abbott repeated. And then . . . I could have sworn he was going to say it, and by golly he did: "There are ladies in the room." I'd have loved it if I hadn't been so scared. There were three eighteenth century Worcester urns made into lamps between Rusty and Brad.

"I should think Brad ought to say what he means," John Michener said quietly. "—Take it easy, Rusty."

"I'll be glad to," Brad said easily. "Rusty's head over heels in debt with his farm, and his wife was signing off. I guess that's clear, isn't it?"

He got up and stood, lithe and flexible, and as wary and ready as a jungle cat.

"In other words, Phyllis wasn't paying the bills after today, and tomorrow morning Rusty's cabbages and all the rest · of his swell front were going to be the laughing stock of Charleston.—And Rusty knew it."

Their eyes held each other's across the sofa, across Mrs. Reid's bowed head, like fused dynamite.

"—And if there's anything you want to settle outside, Lattimer, I'm ready."

"Both of you sit down, or I'll put the bracelets on you," Mr. Abbott said sharply. "Sit down!"

I closed my eyes. It didn't seem possible that hatred could be so naked in two men's eyes. It wasn't decent. I heard a sudden move. "—In a moment now," I thought, but nothing happened. I opened my eyes again. Rusty was sitting down.

74

So was Brad. Nothing else had changed. The score was still to settle.

"Lock that gun room, Colleton," Mr. Michener said. "Give Mr. Abbott the key."

"You needn't bother on my account," Rusty Lattimer said shortly. He didn't say any more, but everybody heard the rest of it. "—I'll kill him with my bare hands."

It was old Doctor John who locked the gun room. Colleton didn't stir from his place beside his mother. If I ever saw murder, it was in his dark face too . . . but for Brad or Rusty or what I couldn't for the life of me have told.

Mr. Abbott took the key of the gun room and put it in his pocket. He stood silently a moment, chewing one corner of his thin wide mouth. Then he said, "You can all go back to town now. You go along with Brad Porter, Doctor John. You stay a minute, Mr. Michener.—You're staying here tonight, Mrs. Baker?"

He looked at Anne.

"I'll stay too," she said quickly.

"All right. You take your mother along now, Mr. Reid. I'd like to see you a minute too, Rusty."

I watched Brad and Doctor John go out, and Colleton and Mrs. Reid. Rusty sat a moment. Then he got up and went out the river door. Anne Latimer got up quickly and went out after him. Mr. Abbott turned to John Michener.

"I declare, Mr. Michener . . . I just can't picture Rusty doing a thing like that."

John Michener started to speak, and looked at me. He shrugged his shoulders. He didn't have to say anything after that. I hurried out of the room. As I got into the hall I heard him say, "Pride and vanity are pretty powerful forces, Chief. They make people do funny things."

. . . And love, I thought, makes them do even funnier things . . . but no one knew that aspect of all this but me. —And Phyllis . . . and she was dead.

12

At the top of the curving stairway I stopped a moment. The door of Phyllis's empty room was closed. The polished floor in front of it was scuffed and clouded from unaccustomed feet. I had a sudden pang of the most acute loneliness. Phyllis, half flower and half poison, always to be coped with, to keep either half from running wild in the garden of my life, was gone, and there was a bare mangled spot where nothing could ever grow again. All the times I could gladly have cut her throat, all the times I had depended on her and she on me to the utmost of friendship, from our perambulators in Rittenhouse Square to . . . to this, came surging back to me.

I crossed blindly to the blue room and closed the door, turned off the light and went and sat in the open window looking out over the gardens. The scattered silver loom of night still glowed up from the river. The stars were far-off fields of yellow crocuses beyond the billowing oak tops. A tree frog croaked, a marsh hen disturbed among the rushes chirped and was lost in the deep silence. Then two figures emerged out of the shadows and out of the silence. Rusty Lattimer and his sister Anne crossed the path. I heard Anne's voice as plainly as if she were in the room with me.

"Don't be a fool, Rusty," she was saying sharply. "You can go away a while. It'll blow over. Plenty of things worse than this have blown over in Charleston. After all, everybody knows you married her for her money. Now you've got it, I don't see what you're stewing about."

They both stopped. Rusty must have been speaking very quietly, because I couldn't hear what he was saying, but I did hear Anne's reply. Her voice was sharp and clear as a bell.

"Oh very well, darling. If that's your story, stick to it. But don't be surprised if nobody else believes it. I'm going to bed. Good night."

She turned and came quickly toward the house, not to the drawing room windows but to the garden door into the hall. Rusty still stood in the garden, watching her. Then he turned abruptly and walked slowly back toward the river.

I heard Anne's light steps on the stairs, heard them hesitate just at the top, at Phyllis's door, then come quickly and stop again, at my door this time. I slipped quietly across the powder blue rug and turned on the bedside light just as a little rap-rap sounded on my door.

"Come in," I called.

I watched the knob turn and the door open. It sounds a little silly, I suppose, but I had a queer feeling that something definitely important to me was happening. And when Anne came in, I knew instantly that something important had happened. I'd suddenly become an unwelcome guest in a stranger's house. It wasn't Phyllis's house any more. Anne Lattimer had taken over. She stood, framed in the door in her long teal-blue evening gown, her cheeks a little flushed, her blue eyes still haggard but with a new light in them . . . the light of possession, I thought unpleasantly. It wasn't itself an awfully pleasant show, someway. It was also something that just hadn't, curiously enough, occurred to me—that Phyllis's death had given Anne Lattimer her second big break . . . just as Rusty's marrying Phyllis had given her her first, the escape from poverty.

I suddenly remembered something Phyllis had said to me five and a half years before in this very room. She'd been standing by the window talking about Rusty. "Oh, he'll marry me, darling. He's crazy about his little sister, and she's plenty smart—and plenty practical—even if she's only twenty-one. And I like her too. I think people ought to be practical. She's got a job in the museum. She'd give her head to have a lot of things she's never had. I rather think she likes me too."

I was remembering that and looking at Anne Lattimer, listening to her saying, "I hope you don't mind terribly. We can send in in the morning for a dress for you to wear back to town, if you can put up with being without your own things tonight. It's stupid of Abbott to put you to all this bother."

"It's quite all right," I said.

"Well, good-night. Let me know if there's anything you want."

"Thank you. Good-night."

She closed the door. I heard her steps along the hall again. I took off my things and put on Phyllis's green and peach velvet negligee. They say life is a series of episodes. I thought as I turned out the light and got into bed that a long one in mine had come to an abrupt and definite end. I lay there thinking in the dark; and suddenly—I don't think it was very long, it couldn't have been—I heard a soft tread in the hall. It stopped very close to my door. I waited.

The door opened quickly. Anne Lattimer was there again. She'd undressed and had on her brother's dressing gown. I could see his pajama legs rolled up about her bare ankles in the light from the hall. I reached for the light as she closed the door and stood leaning against it, her face so bloodless I thought she was going to faint.

I sat up in bed, staring open-mouthed at her.

"I'm awfully sorry!"

She gasped out the words.

"—But I . . . I can't bear to be alone! Would you mind? I'm sorry! I'm . . ."

She looked wild and on the point of hysterics.

"Why don't you sleep here, then?" I said, pointing to the other bed.

"—If you don't mind . . ."

"Not at all."

She didn't look at me. She came quickly across the room and threw off the quilted silk spread.

77

"It's all so awful," she whispered. "I keep seeing her. I just can't bear it."

She collapsed, pale and deadly still, on the bed. I got up and pulled the covers up over her. She buried her head in the pillows. "Poor Rusty!" she moaned. "It's so awful!"

There were a lot of things I might have said, but I didn't.

"Try to go to sleep, Anne," was all I did say. I got back into bed again and turned off the light. I don't know when she went to sleep, or when I did, but I know I woke up again, not sharply but slowly and as perfectly aware as if I'd been awake for hours. I could hear the restless uneven breathing of the girl in the bed beside mine. She moaned uneasily, and turned over, but she was sound asleep, and I knew it was not that that had waked me. I lay there telling myself that every house has its own special sounds at night, and here the silence magnified them, and what I heard was probably only the night wind creeping through the marsh grass up through the old oaks.

But it was no good. The sound I heard was too familiar. It was a dog, his nails scratching on the tile below my window as he bounded about greeting a friend. Yet that friend's footsteps made no sound that I could hear.

I glanced at the pale phosphorescent hands of the clock by my bed. They stood at twenty minutes to four. It had been an hour since Anne had come to my room too terrified to sleep alone. I slipped quietly out of bed, crept across the thick rug and looked out of the open window. There were no lights downstairs. There was no light anywhere . . . Only the dark outline of the oaks and the terrace and the river. I could still hear the dog frisking about happily, and I could hear now the little muffled sounds of joy he was making. Then suddenly it all stopped, and I heard the door close too quietly for a friend to close it.

For a moment I stood, not quite sure that I shouldn't wake Anne. What if it was only Rusty, I thought? But I knew it wasn't. He would have spoken to the dog, told him to lie down . . . and his feet would have made some sound on the tiled porch.

I glanced at the bed beyond mine. I could see the dim outline of covers and hear the same fitful moaning diapason of exhausted sleep. I moved back to my bed, slipped on Phyllis's negligee and heelless slippers, and crept to the door and opened it silently. The hall was dark. I stood there a moment. Some one was on the stairs. I could hear the soft creak of the bannisters and a sharp frightened breath, and then suddenly, as if a yellow ball had dropped and bounced on the polished stair, a light flashed on and off again, and soft feet slipped across the landing and up, and stopped. I heard a hand feel along the panelled door and the soft click of the door opening.

Some one was going into Phyllis's room, and I stood there completely paralyzed, not daring to move or breathe . . . it was all so silent and so stealthy. Then, as suddenly as before, the yellow ball bounced again—on Phyllis's desk between the windows. I heard the little slithering sound of drawers coming out, and saw the light flash into them. They slithered shut again, one after another. I heard the click of the secret drawers that are never secret, saw the yellow light flash into the tambour panel, and a gloved hand slip through it and come out empty.

Then the yellow disc dropped to the bottom drawers, and through each one as it opened, and went off as it was quietly shut again. It jumped then, with the dark hand behind it, like some disembodied thing, moving it on, to Phyllis's dressing table between the river windows, and back again to the satinwood chest of drawers beyond the door to the connecting passage between Phyllis's room and Rusty's. It stood then, moving about the room, searching, it seemed, for still some other place to look, and then it went off suddenly.

I heard a quick movement, the door click softly again, an almost noiseless foot on the stairs, the creak of the bannister, a hand softly touch the wall. Perhaps I should have cried out then, but I didn't . . . for I heard another sound near me, at the end of the hall. Some one else had been watching too. I heard him come now just as I heard the door below open softly and close on velvet hinges.

It was Rusty Lattimer. I knew that by some sixth practical sense that knows when creeping steps belong and when they're alien. He came softly and slowly. I heard his heavier tread on the stairs, his heavier hand creaking the bannisters to the bottom of the stairs . . . but no sound of a door opening or closing, nor did any light go up.

My hand clinging to the door knob was cold, but my heart was colder. I crept back to the window. There was nothing outside there but semi-darkness and silence . . . as profound as death.

I waited there a moment. Then I heard the door on the porch open quietly . . . and I did a very foolish thing. I went back to the door, closed it again and switched on the light. Downstairs I heard a quick sound. The light went on. I went down. Rusty, still dressed, was standing in the door, his face so strange I hardly recognized it.

"I thought I heard something," I said.

"It was just me," he said. "I can't seem to sleep."

I thought: "Then he knew who it was too."

"What do you say we stoke up the fire and have a drink?" he said. "I don't feel like going to bed."

Suddenly there was a noise outside. Bill the English setter bounded up. I stared at him. He was wagging his tail, and in his eyes was the devilish teasing light I thought only a cocker spaniel ever had. In his mouth was a shoe . . . a tan rubber-soled shoe. The tongue was hanging out, and printed on the white lining was "J. R." It was Jennifer's. She'd left it on the porch. And she was somewhere out there now . . . one shoe off and one shoe on. The nursery rhyme rattled grotesquely through my head.

"Drop it, Bill."

Rusty's voice was sharp and unnatural. Bill chastened, let the shoe fall at his master's feet. Rusty picked it up and stuffed the tongue inside.

"One of the Negroes, I guess," he said shortly. He closed the door. I went along to the drawing room. He followed. The fire was still burning a little. He put a piece of lightwood on it, and as it blazed up he tossed the shoe in. The flames caught the leather fringe of the tongue, the sole curled almost as if a living foot and not a man's torn heart was in it.

13

Rusty and I sat there, perfectly silent, watching Jennifer's shoe curl and burn.

"—You think she did it, don't you, Rusty?" I said after a long time.

He looked at me steadily. "I haven't an idea what you're talking about, Diane," he said.

There was a sound behind us. I turned to see Anne Lattimer standing in the door. She was across the room in a flash.

"Rusty! You don't . . . you can't! I didn't do it! I swear I didn't! You can't believe I did!"

Her face was ashy, her eyes unbelievable. Her brother stared at her, limp with shock, and struggled to his feet, blocking out her view of the small shoe still burning there.

"I didn't see her!" Anne cried hysterically. "I was just——"

"Anne!" His voice was like a hand gripping at her throat, choking off something so revealing that it was terrible.

The oddest expression had come into Rusty's eyes. I can't explain what it was exactly, except that for a split second it was hope, and instantly it was something else again . . . dread, or despair.

"For God's sake, pull yourself together," he whispered hoarsely. "Nobody thinks you did it.—Diane, make her go to bed."

He turned away and stood leaning against the mantel. The sole of Jennifer's shoe curled black over the pine logs and fell between the andirons.

I got Anne upstairs. She was in as total a state of collapse as it's possible for any one to be outside a straitjacket, and if I'd had one and known how to use it I'd have put her in it and probably thrown her in the river. All the time I was struggling in my own mind to try to make some of it—any of it—make sense. The only things that were clear at all made not the least. I kept going over them. Jennifer had been in the house. She'd taken the box of Miss Caroline's letters. She'd obviously missed one of them, or more—the most important, or she'd never have run the horrible risk of that last trip. But nothing, not anything in the world, could be so important as that. Not unless—I stopped abruptly there, each time I came to it—not unless her life depended on it.

And if Jennifer was totally inexplicable, Anne Lattimer was more so. Her desperate protest, whether it sprang from guilt or innocence, had still sprung from fear. Everything she'd done all evening simply shrieked of it, now that I watched her, her smooth blonde head buried in the pillow, shaking as if she had malaria. Finally, completely defeated, I went to bed myself and dropped to sleep from sheer exhaustion.

My daytime clothes had come from the Villa next morning when I woke up. With them was a card from Mrs. Atwell Reid. It said: "My dear Mrs. Baker, Will you go over to Strawberry Hill and break the news to Jennifer as early as you can . . . as gently as you can?" It was signed "Elsie Reid."

As I looked up from it I saw Felice standing at the foot of my bed, her black eyes sharpened, fixed on the torn tumbled bed next to mine.

"Mademoiselle Anne had a restless night, n'est-ce pas, madame."

A thin film of ice congealed along my spine. I think at just that moment I became as convinced as the colored servants below stairs that Felice Marin was a devil. How else could anybody make a simple statement of an obvious truth so paralyzing?

"Felice!" I said sharply.

She looked at me with those tight sharp eyes as cold as a snake's.

"All I demand, madame," she said quietly, "is to be allowed to go back to France. She is dead. I warned her. I cannot help what has happened. I only want to go back to

81

France—nothing more. I must have money to go. If you will say that to . . ."

She came to a stop.

"Who shall I say it to, Felice?"

She looked at me, a flicker in her eyes.

"Say it out loud anywhere, madame. They will understand."

"That's what's called blackmail in this country, Felice," I said, as calmly as I could. "It's pretty dangerous."

We looked at each other for a long time.

"I want to go back to France, madame," she said quietly. "Shall I draw madame's tub?"

"Please," I said.

In a moment she was back, putting my slippers together beside my bed. "—I only want to go back to France, madame," she repeated.

I glanced at her sharply. The unveiled threat that had been in those words before was gone. There was nothing in them now but the most profound and poignant nostalgia; they were a cry from a lonely, unutterably lonely, heart.

"They do not like foreigners here," she said as she closed the door behind her.

"They certainly don't," I thought . . . and "foreigner" is more relative a term in Charleston than anywhere else in the world outside of Richmond, I should imagine. Not for nothing can a tombstone here read "Sacred to the memory of of ———, who lived in our midst for seventy-five years, our most beloved stranger." Phyllis had battered her head against that, and I had the notion I was being asked to do much the same now, as I looked again at Mrs. Reid's note. Nevertheless, I wanted to see Jennifer. I got dressed and started to go out into the hall, and stopped. I could hear the slow kindly voice of John Michiner, and Mr. Abbott's, slow but hardly kindly. They were in Phyllis's room across the hall.

"It's bound to make a stink, Mr. Michener."

"It doesn't have to pollute the whole country, Abbott. If we can keep the divorce business under our hats, for instance . . ."

"That's just what we can't do," Mr. Abbott replied. "Not with this fellow Brad out for Lattimer's blood like he is."

They were both silent for a moment.

"It beats me how anybody could walk in, with a crowd of people around," Mr. Abbott went on, "with a long string of moss in his hand, and nobody notice it. He must have got it from the avenue and come straight up here. They tell me downstairs Miz' Latimer had most of it taken off the trees this side . . . it gave her the creeps, she said. And they were all out in back, except you and this Brad."

"I'm afraid I killed a very rich client, in case you think I did it," John Michener said composedly. "As for Brad, he expected to marry the girl again. People don't cut off their noses so thoughtlessly these lean years, frankly."

"Not unless they're fools . . . or drunk," Mr. Abbott said. "They tell me he's been hittin' the bottle right hard lately."

There was another silence.

"No," he said slowly; "it don't look so hot for Rusty. But *good God,* Mr. Michener, I've known that boy's family all my life."

The door closing on that sentence was symbolic, in some way, of the whole investigation that was to follow. It seemed to me that every time they came to an avenue that would seem open they closed it quietly, saying, "*Good God,* I've known that family all my life," and that settled that. Yet somehow I trusted John Michener, trusted him where I wouldn't have trusted any of the official policemen.

I slipped downstairs and through the empty hall, and stopped on the river porch, startled for a moment by the contradiction of it all: the blue river beyond the golden fringe of marsh, the flaming banks of azaleas and the golden first yellow of the live oaks, silvered high up with pale streaming moss. It wasn't the setting for murder. I looked up at the sky. A single buzzard in the blue intense altitude wheeled a grim denial that death was not as present here as anywhere.

I went on through the old rose garden, white with early silver moons, came to the long arbor of wisteria, foaming like purple and violet spray in the soft breeze, and followed straight on to where the fringe of green wood began, yellow with tangled jessamines and white and magenta-flecked with dogwood and Judas tree. There was a bridle path there, and I kept to it until I came to a huge oak in a sudden clearing . . . a giant Laocoön stained pale green with lichen and bearded hoary with great thick streamers of moss. On the thick green grass about its roots, coiled like scaly serpents' backs, was a pile of moss. It didn't lie rolled as if the wind had blown it, or clinging, a feathery cocoon, to a piece of dead branch as if it had fallen there. It was torn from a low branch . . . the single strands still hanging like ravelled threads above it.

I stood for a long time looking down at it. Then I bent over, picked it up and tossed it up into the tree, my hands shaking a little.

Not far beyond the oak the path wound down to the river bank, and suddenly I could see Miss Caroline's chimneys, the white gate and the high green wall of camellias. In front of the gate was a moss-dripped oak, and under it a grey tomb, its crumbling heraldic sculpture sprigged with delicate fern and goat's beard, brown fungus indenting the figures "1692" carved over the door. Jennifer had had to pass this,

83

back to the desolate mangled house whose secret she kept locked tight in the tomb of her own heart.

I pushed the gate open and went out of the jungle into the prim garden. An old colored woman smoking a cherry pipe looked at me with shuttered hostile eyes.

"Nobody home," she said flatly.

"Tell Miss Jennifer that Mrs. Baker is here, and that I'd like to see her."

She shook her head. "Don't nobody live here."

Just then the door opened behind her and Jennifer came out. Her blue eyes were bigger, it seemed to me, deep-sapphire blue with their fringing of long black lashes, and her face was pale, almost magnolia-white under her mop of short curly black hair. I'd expected that. But there was something else that disturbed me. I couldn't place it exactly. It was a kind of overtone or undertone that came out of the faintly drooping lines of her young body, as if the fear had been deeper and the release from it even greater than she'd known.

"I've heard about it," she said evenly.

"Your mother asked me to come and break the news gently."

We sat down on the steps, Jennifer looking straight ahead of her across the garden to the river.

"—Did you find my shoe?" she asked quietly.

I didn't answer that. "I saw you leave the house with your aunt's leather box."

She still didn't look at me, but two spots of color burned over her cheek bones.

"Then I can expect the police any minute now?"

"No," I said. "I haven't told them. And no one knows it."

"Some one does," she said. There was a little catch in her voice. "Somebody was in the arbor as I came through."

"Who?"

"I don't know. It doesn't matter.—You see, they weren't her papers. My aunt had to have them back. . . . She *had* to," she repeated, her low voice vibrating with sudden warmth. "They were her . . . intimate papers. She was almost out of her mind when she found they were gone."

It was difficult to imagine the little old lady in that time-stilled room above us as anything but calm and self-contained.

"It was pretty awful, really," Jennifer said. "I've never seen her disturbed or upset, ever in my life. She has a kind of . . . inner peace. She has a quality nobody else has. And I'd . . . I guess it sounds funny, Diane, but . . . well, there's not anything I wouldn't do to keep any one from destroying. it. Not anything."

I didn't dare look at her. Only the very young can be so passionate and so selfless and so serious without seeming naïve and humorless. And I was rather more disturbed too, way down in the pit of my stomach, than I wanted to admit. "Anything," the way she said it, meant just that. And Phyllis Lattimer was dead.

"I can't understand Phyllis not giving the papers up," I said, after we'd sat there silently for a while. "Did you ask her for them?"

"I met her coming back to Darien, when I was on my way to get them. Aunt Caroline had started to tell me something. We were talking about marriage. She hadn't brought up what Phyllis said about Brad. I hoped she'd forgotten it, because . . . well, it wasn't true, of course. I mean, I like Brad, but he doesn't want to marry me, and I certainly don't want to marry him.—Aunt Caroline was in love with Doctor John."

She hesitated. "You've heard about it?"

I nodded. She looked at me with wide serious blue eyes.

"If you live alone in the past, things in the past don't die. Aunt Caroline still reads his letters. She can't see them, and the ink's faded, but she knows the feel of them, and she knows every word in them by heart. When she asks for that box, it almost breaks my heart."

She turned her head away quickly.

"Yesterday she said, 'If you are very much in love, Jennifer, I don't think divorce should stand in the way. There are worse tragedies, my dear, than divorce. Will you hand me my box?' I got it. I couldn't tell her it wasn't Brad, just then . . ."

I nodded. I could still see her the other day when Miss Caroline spoke of her marriage and her children.

"I got her the box. When she opened it, she was so pale I thought she'd . . . gone. Then she said, 'Jenny, you must get that other box. Mrs. Lattimer took . . . the wrong one. You must get it at once, child . . . at once, do you hear?' "

Her fingers trembled a little.

"Phyllis was driving in the gate as I drove out ours. I told her my aunt had found she'd taken the wrong box by mistake, and could I come up and get it. She said, 'No.' Then she laughed. 'My dear child, your aunt's material is priceless. Charleston will simply love it.' I didn't know what to do. I said, 'I'm sorry, but my aunt wants it back.' She said, 'Darling, tell your aunt I can well imagine she wants it back . . . but she's not going to get it—not till I'm through with it.' She went on, and just then mother drove up. I shouldn't have told her, but I did. She said she'd see Phyllis. I came back and waited, and then drove back down to the gate. A colored boy told me mother'd gone back to town. I drove to the service station by St. Andrew's and phoned. She said she'd talked to Phyllis, and she thought I was making a mountain out of a molehill; that Phyllis would return the letters before dinner."

. "And what did you do?" I asked.

"What could I do?" she said helplessly. "I came back and told Aunt Caroline mother had seen Phyllis and she'd send the box. Aunt Caroline said, 'Your mother is a fool.' She's never liked her very much, you know. She had me get her paper and a pen and wrote a note, and sent Rachel's boy over to Darien. He came back and said Mark had taken the note to Phyllis, and she'd return the box as soon as it was convenient—she had guests."

Her blue eyes stared wide open out across the garden to the winding river.

"I know this sounds unreal," she said.

"Maybe your mother doesn't know about Doctor John's letters."

"Oh yes she does," Jennifer replied shortly . . . so shortly that I was a little startled. "She just doesn't realize you can't go on forever playing both ends against the middle."

She was silent a moment. Then she said, "Don't think I'm not fond of my mother, and that I don't feel terribly sorry for her. I do.—She was in love with John Michener, you know, and she married father. And after father . . . died, people thought mother and John would marry. But I guess if you've been in love and got over it, it doesn't ever come back."

We'd got away from the business of the letters. But she didn't have to tell me the rest about them. I could imagine very well the hours that had elapsed in the room upstairs until Jennifer had at last gone over after them herself.

Then she said, "When I got home with Aunt Caroline's box she was too faint to do anything but nod and keep patting it almost as if it was a baby she'd lost and got back. And I was just getting ready to go to bed when I heard a car out in front. I was terrified. I knew they'd come . . . after me. I put on my dressing gown over my dress and came down-stairs."

I stared at her open-mouthed.

"It was Brad," she whispered. "He came to tell me Phyllis was dead. I don't know why. He hadn't seen me . . . because I'd seen him."

My heart was a cold heavy lump in the pit of my stomach. It was the note, Miss Caroline's note that I'd held wadded in the palm of my hand, that had brought Brad Porter over to Strawberry Hill.

"He just stood on the porch, in front, looking at me," Jennifer went on. "Then he said, 'Phyllis is dead, Jennifer. The police have been out, they've taken her away to Charleston. I thought you'd want to know.' "

She didn't look at me.

86

"I went back upstairs. Aunt Caroline was sitting up in bed. All the papers were out of the box, scattered all over the counterpane. 'They're gone, Jennifer, they're not here!' she kept saying, over and over again. 'You must get them, at once. It's important!' "

She stopped. "—That's why I went back," she said simply.

"Did you find them?"

She shook her head. "I didn't know where to look. I had to come away without them, because I saw a light go on upstairs. I got back here and sat down in the hall for a minute. Then, all of a sudden, I saw something under the door. It was a packet of letters—some one had put them there."

"When?" I asked.

"I don't know. I hadn't seen them till then. I took them upstairs. Aunt Caroline cried—it's the first time I've ever seen her cry. Then she held one of them out to me, and told me to read it. There was a note with it—she told me to read that too."

Her voice was no louder than the whispering wind in the pine tops.

"—You must understand, Diane! You know Phyllis— there wasn't any other way! Oh, how I wish there had been!"

I've never heard a cry so low and poignant, or so heart-breakingly resolute. She bent her dark head forward, her hands gripped tightly in her lap. Suddenly she straightened up like a shot, listening, her red lips parted a little, her face paler.

"—Somebody's coming," she whispered.

She heard the car a full minute before I did.

"Don't you padlock the gate any more?" I asked.

"I left it open for mother yesterday. I usually leave it open when I'm home, anyway."

She was still listening, glancing now at the garden gate. It swung open in a moment and Brad Porter came through.

14

He hesitated an instant, seeing me sitting there, before he came on. I had the feeling that he'd have preferred my not being there, and started to get up.

"Don't go . . . please," Jennifer said quickly. "—Hello, Brad."

"Hello, Jennifer . . . Diane."

He looked like a man who'd planned under other circumstances to say something quite different. He stood a little awkwardly, fishing for a pack of cigarettes.

"Have they found out anything yet, Brad?"

"I don't think they want to find out very much," he said shortly. He shrugged. "Abbott and your friend John Michener had me on the carpet this morning."

"What for?" I asked. Jennifer's blue eyes had shuttered ever so warily.

"It seems they don't believe Phyllis was going to marry me again, when she'd divorced Rusty."

Jennifer stiffened . . . and I was appalled. She hadn't, of course, heard any of that.

"Divorce?"

"Rusty didn't know it either, did he?" I asked quickly. Then I realized that that was wrong. Whatever the answer was, Rusty Lattimer was on the spot. If he knew, then he murdered her to keep her from divorcing him. If he didn't, then he murdered her because she wouldn't. Assuming, of course, that he hadn't a thousand other good and sufficient reasons for doing it.

Brad looked at me silently for a moment. "I'm interested in this for two reasons," he said then. "Three, to be frank, but since we're not being, we won't go into the third. First, I was pretty fond of Phyllis, and I'd like to see the guy that did this get what's coming to him. Second . . ."

His eyes met mine steadily.

"—Or I guess you'd put it first, pal . . . I don't want the local Gestapo pinning this on the first ex-husband they get their hands on. So I'm not just a disinterested bystander. And what's more, I think there's something screwy about the whole setup, and I'm going to bust it wide open."

He looked down at Jennifer. She'd sat quite still for a long time, her eyes fixed, unseeing, in front of her. She looked up at him. Their eyes held a long minute.

"Why don't you loosen up, sister? You know all about it, don't you?"

"No," Jennifer said. Only the sharp throb of the pulse in her throat showed she'd been steeling herself against that.

"I guess they don't teach little girls at St. Michael's what happens to them if they don't tell the truth," Brad said. "Well, I'll shove. You aren't coming, Diane—or are you?"

I got up. "Yes, I think I am," I said. "Good-bye, Jennifer." At the gate through the clipped wall of glossy-leaved camellias I looked back. She was still standing at the foot of the steps watching us.

Neither Brad nor I spoke until we were halfway down the avenue, airy mauve and smoke-grey with the morning sun streaking through the silver-tinselled live oaks.

"I thought Phyllis was cockeyed when she said that kid was out after Rusty," Brad remarked soberly.

"I think she was," I said.

"You wouldn't try to fool me, would you, honey?"

"No," I answered. "I'm not saying I don't think she's in love with him. I'm saying I don't think she was out after him."

He nodded, to my surprise.

"That's the weak point in the old capacity-for-sacrifice theory. If you've got it, somebody's always going to let you use it. That's what they're doing to Jennifer."

"You aren't turning into a White Knight before my very eyes, are you?" I inquired.

"It's just a touch of the local *mal des fleurs*," Brad said easily. "Too many azaleas, too much wisteria, and too much Low Country applesauce strained too thin."

"You'd better go back North," I said. "First thing you know you'll be wanting to marry the girl."

He shook his head. "She couldn't afford me, Diane."

"I think you're a complete louse, Brad," I said.

"Just a realist, Diane.—You want to go on up to Darien?"

"I suppose I ought to," I said. "I'm about as popular as the cholera."

"Little Anne?"

I nodded. "She's another of you realists."

He shrugged. "She's scared pea-green, is all. And don't have a heart to heart talk about Jennifer with her."

I must have looked a little startled.

"Anne thinks it's Jennifer's fault Colleton doesn't marry her," Brad went on.

"Why on earth?"

"Because if Jennifer would persuade old Miss Caroline to go into town, and sell Strawberry Hill and the stuff in it, everything would be lovely. They say the furniture and pictures are priceless."

"Oh," I said.

"Maybe she's right. Anyway, they're all pretty sore, about the way Jennifer guards the old lady and won't let anybody near her. I guess Anne knows that when Miss Caroline dies, Colleton won't even get a gout stool out of the place.—You know about him killing his father there?"

I nodded. "—Is that why Anne's so scared now?"

"I shouldn't be surprised. Actually, of course, Colleton's the one person who hadn't any reason for doing away with Phyllis."

"What do you mean?"

"She was going to smoke Jenny and old Miss out of Strawberry Hill. She and Anne and Mrs. Reid had it all fixed. Then

Anne and Colleton could get married and all would be swell. Wasn't that what Phyl got you down here for?"

"Something of the sort," I said. "And why doesn't he marry Anne anyway?"

"Money," Brad said laconically. "He can't afford to marry and support his mother too. That's why Mrs. Reid is so anxious to sell the place. Also she told me once that if somebody bought it and got it out of the way as a romantic tragic spot, so people weren't always talking about it, he'd get over it. He was only fifteen when it happened, not legally responsible actually."

"I wonder if anybody can ever forget killing anybody," I said.

He didn't answer for a while. He was looking through the windshield up Phyllis's lovely avenue of oaks.

"You think it would always haunt you?"

"You could wipe it off the surface of your mind, I should think," I said. "But I shouldn't think whoever murdered Phyl could ever really forget it. When he walked under the moss . . ."

"For God's sake, shut up!" Brad said hoarsely. His face was quite pale under the deep sun tan.

He let in the clutch abruptly, and we shot forward into the oak avenue. A long streamer of moss hit against the windshield. As he swerved the car a little to avoid it, I shuddered. I knew that even for me the silvery grey and dark blackish-green tendrils would never be things of light and air again. I'd always see them in a thick lethal wad on a girl's face . . . and torn from a single great oak in a clearing in the spring woods not far from a lichen-covered tomb beside a blind and desolate house.

There were three cars in the drive in front of the portico of Darien. As Brad drew up to let me out, Mr. Abbott, John Michener and Doctor John came out of the house, Doctor John in his rusty-green black coat, ancient panama and flamboyant black ribbon tie looking infinitely old and fragile and tenuous.

"I'd like to speak to you, Mrs. Baker," Mr. Abbott said. "Will you step into the library, please."

Brad waved to me, spun around in the drive, and disappeared down the avenue. I went inside and through the door at the right. On the library mahogany desk between the two front windows was a sheaf of mail, thin magazines mostly with cows and chickens on the covers and advertisements from farm supply houses. It hadn't been touched, and lay there a significant little island in the cypress-panelled room. Mr. Abbott closed the door and sat on the edge of the old desk, looking at the end of his cigar.

90

"You saw a good deal of Mrs. Lattimer the last three days, I believe, Mrs. Baker," he said. "I understand she telegraphed for you to come down. What for?"

I hesitated. I didn't want to blaze a trail straight to Strawberry Hill, and I hadn't thought up anything to say.

"We were very old friends," I got out, a little lamely, I suppose.

"You mean she didn't have anything special on her mind?"

I shook my head.

Mr. Abbott pulled a telegram out of his pocket. "She wired you, 'Come down instantly darling I need you terribly love Phyllis,' " he said. "Surely, Mrs. Baker, that looks like she had something on her mind . . . ?"

"If you knew Phyllis Lattimer, it wouldn't sound so," I said.

"But it sounded urgent enough to you to make you fly down the next day, Mrs. Baker."

"I always fly if there aren't any mountains in the way," I retorted.

He frowned. "She wanted you to come down because she was having trouble with her husband . . . wasn't that it?"

"It certainly was not," I said. "The whole divorce business came out of a clear sky, so far as I'm concerned. It was a bolt from the blue."

"But you told Mr. Michener she told you she was going to get a divorce?"

"That was yesterday afternoon, after she'd seen him. I couldn't have been more surprised."—Which was true, certainly . . . surprised and incredulous.

Mr. Abbott leaned forward.

"Mrs. Baker . . . are you asking me to believe you and Mrs. Latimer—old friends as you were—spent those three days together without her telling you all her troubles and just what she figured on doing?"

"I'm not asking you to believe anything, Mr. Abbott," I said. "I'm merely telling you she did not tell me until after she went into Charleston yesterday that she intended divorcing Rusty."

"She didn't tell you she was opposed to this farming idea of Lattimer's?"

"She's always regarded that as a bit of amiable idiocy."

He looked at me a long time.

"You were here at dinner night before last, I understand?"

My heart sank. I nodded.

"You didn't hear the knock-down drag-out they had . . . that ended with him leaving the house and not coming back all night? The Frenchwoman heard it. It's funny you didn't."

"They had a set-to," I said. "Is there any married couple that doesn't?"

"Most of them don't have set-tos that end in murder, Mrs. Baker," Mr. Abbott remarked placidly. "Not down here they don't."

"They were on very good terms in the evening when I came out," I said, as convincingly as I could . . . and instantly realized that that was a mistake. He caught me up at once.

"—After she'd ploughed up his fields and made arrangements to get a divorce, Mrs. Baker? Without telling him about either, if we're to believe what he says?"

He looked at me steadily. "And there's one other thing. Maybe you won't be so chary talking about it. This Frenchwoman, Felice. What do you know about her?"

"Nothing," I said. "Except that she's been with Mrs. Lattimer ten years or more. She was loyal and efficient, and got on very well with her."

He looked at me again, for an uncomfortably long time. Then he got up. "Just call me, Mrs. Baker, when you decide there's no use beating about the bush any longer. I guess you don't know murder's a dangerous business. If I was you, I'd watch my step. Maybe you could know too much, Mrs. Baker. Wouldn't like to see anything happen to you down here."

He closed the door.

I was disturbed—I didn't want anything to happen to me either—but I was annoyed too. I should have had a more plausible explanation of Phyllis's telegram. I hadn't, of course, thought it was terribly urgent, simply because I'd thought it *was* going to be husband trouble, and while Phyllis might have thought it urgent—it was urgent if Phyllis wanted a glass of water—I knew it wasn't, really. And I *had* flown because I prefer to get anywhere as quickly as possible. But if I'd told him frankly what Phyllis really wanted, Jennifer's house of cards would have fallen . . . and still in my ears I could hear that "Not while she's alive! I can't, I can't!"

I crossed the hall into the drawing room. It was empty except for Mark, the colored butler. He gave me a sullen sidelong glance and started out.

"Is Mr. Lattimer around, Mark?" I asked.

"He's in there, miss." He pointed toward the gun room. It occurred to me suddenly that they'd unlocked it now Brad was gone. The door was slightly open, I saw as I crossed the drawing room. I put out my hand to push it wide open, and stopped abruptly as Anne Lattimer's voice, raised and sharp-edged, struck my ears.

"—All right. If you won't tell them, I will. I'll——"

"You'll do nothing of the kind," Rusty Lattimer's voice

92

cut in curtly. "You'll keep your mouth shut. Understand? Her name's not going to be mentioned. She's not going to be in it."

"Look here, Rusty." Her voice was like an icicle. "What's going on? You're not in love with Jennifer Reid, are you?"

"I told you to keep her out of this," Rusty said dangerously.

"—Don't you know that Jennifer's in love with Brad . . . and don't you know Phyllis was divorcing you so *she* could marry Brad? And Brad wasn't having any? Why do you suppose he got stinko last night?"

She laughed shortly.

"Because he wants to marry Jennifer . . . and Phyllis had him cornered! She's been seeing him all along. She always thought he was perfectly safe . . . until Jennifer came along! And she was chucking you because she wasn't letting Jennifer have him. Everybody in town knows it but you. And they know about Brad and Jennifer. Jennifer doesn't give a damn about you except as her tenant farmer."

I didn't hear what Rusty said. I slipped back across the room and out into the hall again, and stood there, more disturbed and more confused by all these conflicting cross-currents than I'd been at any time before. I heard a quiet step at the end of the hall and glanced around. Felice, her black eyes like a pair of storm signals, halted abruptly. Then she came forward, every inch the lady's maid again except for those angry eyes.

"Is madame staying for lunch?"

I shook my head. There might have been a lot of things I wasn't sure of, but I was sure of one: I wanted to get away from Darien instantly and never come back as long as I lived.

I went quickly out onto the pink-washed flagstones. Mr. Abbott, John Michener and old Doctor John were standing by Mr. Michener's car, talking earnestly. I looked back. Felice was flying up the stairs on soundless feet. Something cold stirred inside me. She'd always been a strange sort of person—now she seemed to me a definitely enigmatic and even terrifying one.

I hurried across to the three men. "Are you going into town, Mr. Michener?" I asked. "Could I go with you?"

"Sure, Miss Diane. It will be a pleasure."

I got in. The car moved around the drive and under the oak avenue, Doctor John beside Mr. Michener in front.

"I've been wanting to speak to you, Miss Diane," Mr. Michener said. I caught his eyes in the mirror . . . kindly but so shrewd and searching as you wouldn't believe. "I'm interested in Brad.—Phyllis talked to you. Did you get the idea she intended marrying him again?"

93

"No, I certainly did not," I said.

"Well, she talked to me at considerable length yesterday in my office. I asked her what she planned to do after she divorced Rusty. She said she had no plans. She didn't mention Brad at all. In fact, I can't believe she had the remotest intention of marrying him again."

"I can't either," I said. "There wasn't any adventure in things she knew."

He nodded. "That's why I can't quite . . . well, it makes Brad's story interesting."

I suddenly thought of something then. The little old gentleman sitting in the front seat had left Darien with Brad the night before. That meant he must have gone to Strawberry Hill with him too. Did Mr. Michener know that, I wondered? I wanted to ask, and I didn't dare. I still wanted to keep all of it away from Strawberry Hill as long as I could.

We crossed the Ashley River bridge, turned into Ashley Avenue and left along Broad Street. Mr. Michener pulled up at the post office curb. "I'll let you out here, if you don't mind," he said deliberately. "There's Brad now . . . going into my office, I expect."

I glanced across Charleston's Mason and Dixon's line. Brad's tall figure was disappearing into the narrow square. Suddenly I felt as if I'd got involved in a game of cat and mouse. I looked at the little doctor, chattering Gullah to a grinning old Negress, her kinky head turbaned and stuck with sulphur matches to keep the ghosts away. If I could only understand him, I kept thinking. Why hadn't he told them he and Brad had gone to Strawberry Hill? He couldn't have known Jennifer had been at Darien. Was he too, I wondered, wearing a sulphur match in his hair . . . keeping a modern specter away from the old ghost-ridden house in the jungle of moss and oak and magnolia?

——Man brings nothing into this world, he can take nothing out of it . . . The words, intoned in the crowded hushed walls of St. Michael's, beat their moving cadence in my ears. The eighth commandment, gold-blazoned above the chancel rail, left an after-image on the retina of my mind. Phyllis had taken nothing out of the world, but she had left a terrible shadow in it. I sat, head bowed, in the box pew beside Rusty and Anne Lattimer. Mr. Abbott's eyes moved, like little snakes', from face to face in the darkened church. It seemed indecent, someway; and the thing that disturbed me chiefly he didn't seem aware of . . . the white marble-hard face of the girl who sat beside her mother, her eyes on the prayer book in her lap.

Jennifer, I thought, hadn't wanted to come here. And when it was over, and I went back to the house in Landgrave Street, she was there, and I knew again she hadn't wanted to be there either. We left together, she and I. Her shabby car was parked down toward the Battery, and we walked along, saying nothing till we got to it.

Perhaps it was what Brad had said, perhaps something else, but all during the day I'd been worried about Jennifer. As we came to the car I said,

"I'm being pretty officious, Jennifer . . . but I don't like to think of you at Strawberry Hill by yourself. If Brad's right, and you do know more about . . . all this than you're telling, it isn't safe."

"No one knows I know," she said quietly. "Brad was just taking a shot in the dark. Anyway, if they did know——"

Her voice caught a little.

"——I'd be perfectly safe. It . . . it doesn't concern me, any of it . . . really."

I looked at her. She did know, then . . . and if Brad had just taken a shot in the dark he'd hit something; and a wounded thing in the dark is a dangerous thing.

She looked back at me, her eyes clear and wide.

"You don't understand, Diane. It isn't a simple thing. You mustn't ever tell any one what Brad said. It isn't safe for you. And I can't ever tell. If I do know, nothing in the world would make me say I know."

"Nothing?"

She shook her head.

"Not even if the evidence Mr. Abbott's piling up against Rusty——"

She turned her face quickly so I couldn't see it.

"Oh, don't!" she whispered. "It wasn't Rusty! He had nothing to do with it! You mustn't say such a terrible thing!"

"I'm not saying it," I said evenly. "Mr. Abbott is, Brad is. All I'm saying is, will you let them go on saying it . . . until it's too late, and Rusty's——"

She stopped me with a quick desperate hand on my arm.

"You don't understand, Diane!" she cried, her voice intense and vibrating from its very roots. "I can't help myself. There's nothing I can do, *nothing*—no matter *what* they do!"

"Not even if they send him to prison . . . or the electric chair?"

"Not even then," she whispered. "Not *anything!* And Rusty'd understand!"

15

Jennifer released my arm abruptly. She was looking down the street, and her eyes had shuttered as instantly as if some one had closed the blinds of a tragic room.

I glanced around. Her brother Colleton and Doctor John were coming toward us. Jennifer opened the door of her car and got in, and then, as if she might as well face it, put the key in the ignition and waited. Colleton nodded to me and leaned forward.

"Look, Jennifer," he said brusquely. "Why don't you get Mrs. Baker to go out and stay with you tonight? You look all in."

"I'll be glad to," I said.

"Colleton's right, Jennifer," Doctor John put in.

A flicker of alarm shot through the girl's eyes. I knew she didn't want me out there. They hadn't any right forcing her to seem rude and ungracious.

"Why don't you drive me round to the Villa?" I said. "We can talk it over."

Colleton's dark eyes met mine for an instant. "Mother doesn't think Jennifer ought to be out there alone," he said curtly.

"It's quite unwise," Doctor John said. He was like a withered Greek chorus in the background, with his flamboyant tie, the soft breeze moving the silky white hair of his uncovered head, his ancient panama resting on the gold head of his cane.

Jennifer reached over and opened the car door, and I got in. We moved off, leaving the two men standing there. She didn't look at me. She said, "You must think I'm very rude."

I shook my head. "But if you could stand it, I think you'd be wise to have somebody out there with you, in spite of everything."

"This is different," she said quietly. "And . . . well, you mightn't be safe, if anybody thought . . ."

She shook her head slowly.

"——Will you be furious if I ask you one thing?" I said.

She looked at me, her eyes widening, wondering—you could see—"Is the blow going to fall now?"

"What is it?" she asked.

"Are you in love with Brad?"

She stared at me, completely surprised. "No, of course not. Wherever did you get that idea?"

"Oh, I just got it," I said.

She laughed. "And Brad's not in love with me. He was in love with Phyllis. That was his only interest in me."

"What do you mean?"

She didn't answer for a moment; she sat there running her gloved forefinger around the wheel. Suddenly she said, "Phyllis wanted you to try to get Aunt Caroline's furniture for her, didn't she?"

I nodded.

"Brad's been trying to get it too," she said. "He doesn't know I know it. He never mentioned Phyllis."

Her red mouth twisted in a wry little smile.

"Well," she went on abruptly, "the point is, Diane—there isn't any furniture. Only what you saw. There's no panelling even . . . except what you saw."

I didn't say anything. There was nothing I could say.

"——Or did you guess it?"

"Vaguely," I admitted.

"Did *you* tell her?"

The faint emphasis on the "you" interested me.

"No," I said. "I didn't."

"I wonder how she found it out?" Jennifer asked.

"Does Brad know?"

"No, I'm sure he doesn't. He's never been in the house—and if he had he wouldn't have known. Only somebody with a feeling about houses would know. That's why I didn't want you to come out."

"Do many people know it?"

She shook her head. "Rusty—but he wouldn't have told her. Anne doesn't. Nobody does except us—Colleton and mother and me."

She hesitated again. ". . . Except Doctor John. He must know. He's never said so . . . only he bought the ribband back chair at a sale in New York. That's how we happened to have it. He just came out with it one day and left it. Of course, Aunt Caroline doesn't know.—That's the whole point."

The color burned, a dull faint shadow, in her face and throat.

"She can't ever know, you see," she said simply.

"Who sold it?" I asked.

"Mother. She had to, of course. My father invested Aunt Caroline's money and his own, and lost practically every bean of it. Mother didn't know it until after he . . . died. Aunt Caroline idolized him, and mother didn't dare tell her."

"But how could she sell the things without your aunt knowing?"

"Aunt Caroline was in the hospital. I think mother didn't think she'd ever come out. She was over seventy, and so delicate. We needed the money horribly. When they found out Aunt Caroline was going to get well, mother was almost frantic. She couldn't tell her . . . it would have killed her. And then it turned out Aunt Caroline couldn't ever walk but a step or two again, so she could never go downstairs. And mother kept putting off telling her until it was too late to do it, ever."

She hesitated.

"Mother should have told her in the beginning, but she didn't. I guess any lie is like a snowball . . . after a while it gets so big you can't let it go without its crushing you. Aunt Caroline is very old. It's an awful thing to say, but I know mother keeps praying she'll die and release her. I feel so desperately sorry for both of them."

There was something very poignant and moving in the low vibrant registers of her voice.

"You see, I was there, you know, when my father died. They sent Colleton away to school. Nobody ever said anything. Then one day at my school a girl a little older than I was got provoked with me for something. She said 'My brother's not a murderer, like yours.' Aunt Caroline taught me after that—I never went back to school."

"Children are so horribly cruel," I said.

She smiled unhappily. "It's what they call tragic irony, I guess. Because it was Anne Lattimer said that. Irony, I mean, that she had to grow up and fall in love with Colleton."

"Does he know it? That she said it, I mean?"

She shook her head.

"He was away at school. I never told any one but Aunt Caroline. It was too terrible. I never even told her who it was said it. And I don't suppose Anne remembers it. That was before Aunt Caroline was sick and mother sold the things.

". . . And even that's not all," she went on after a moment. "Aunt Caroline doesn't know Darien was sold. She thinks mother built a small house on it and Phyllis rents it."

"How can she?" I asked. "Didn't she have to sign papers?"

She nodded. "But she's quite blind. She thought she was signing a long lease.—Oh, it isn't as terrible as it sounds, Diane. I mean what mother did. She had to—don't you see? To keep Aunt Caroline and Colleton and me from starving. We hadn't any money at all. And I know she thought it was only a year or two at the most before all the property would be ours."

"And instead it's been eleven."

"And may be eleven more. And mother doesn't know now that Aunt Caroline's made another will. It's all right, because she's left everything to me, and I'll share what's left."

"Does Colleton know about that?" I asked.

"Yes. I thought he ought to, and he understands. You see, we've spent all our lives taking care of mother and Aunt Caroline. It's been a staggering responsibility. You can't imagine how difficult adults are, these days."

A quick smile flashed through her eyes and lighted her face with an infectious gaiety that I'd never have suspected, completely transforming her.

"So you see," she said, "that's why I'm ungracious and inhospitable about Strawberry Hill, and that's why I keep the doors and windows barred and the gate padlocked. It isn't because I can't stand my mother and I'm trying to get all my aunt's property for myself, the way you'll hear if you stay around a while."

Under her calm there was a wistful quality I hadn't thought of her as having. She was just a child, really. It struck me suddenly what years of loneliness she'd spent out there in that desolate house, living in constant fear of trespassers and of friends too, alive and warm and young in a company of ghosts, dead ghosts and live ones . . . without a single sulphur match in her curly blue-black hair to save her from them.

"Well," I said, "I'm going to Strawberry Hill with you if I have to sleep on the hall sofa. Come along. I'll get a tooth brush and we'll go. And don't be silly."

"But it's so primitive!"

"Darling, I'm just so Spartan it's nauseating."

"It'll come in handy at Strawberry Hill."

She said that with her quick radiant smile. I didn't wonder that Rusty was in love with her. He must have been the only one who'd got much of a glimpse of her not always on guard against the avalanche, alone with her in the river garden.

She switched on the ignition and let in the clutch. We rounded the driveway into South Battery and drew up in front of the Villa. I saw the quick change in her eyes as we stopped. Anne Lattimer was coming down the white steps. For a moment we both thought—I suppose both hoped—she'd pass without seeing us. But she didn't. She crossed the parking strip to the car, looking unhappier, I thought, than any human being I'd ever seen.

"I came to ask you to come back out to Darien, Diane," she said. Her voice had the warm cordiality of a fly inviting a spider to lunch. "Rusty wants you especially. I'm sorry if I seemed rude last night."

She was looking at me but seeing Jennifer. The anxiety in her eyes was not concerned with me in any way.

"She's coming to Strawberry Hill to stay with me," Jennifer said calmly.

99

Anne's jaw dropped.

"The Villa's too luxurious," Jennifer added, by way of explanation.

"It's kind of you," I said. "If there's anything I can do . . ."

"I'll . . . tell him," Anne said blankly. She hesitated a minute, looking at Jennifer. "Has . . . Mr. Abbott been around to see your mother?"

Jennifer's face was a little pale. "I don't know. Was he . . . ?"

"Felice had a long talk with him while we were at lunch. Mark heard her telling him that a box of papers Phyllis had was missing . . . and that she'd heard your mother and Phyllis having a row about them in the afternoon, and your mother'd flown out of the house very much upset."

There was a little silence.

"Felice's crazy," Jennifer said.

"She may be," Anne replied. "But she's making a frightful lot of trouble. She told Abbott that the night before Rusty had asked Phyllis to divorce him, and she'd refused, and Rusty stormed out of the house and didn't come back all night. And Phyllis had said she'd see him in hell before she'd divorce him, and nothing could make Felice believe she'd changed her mind."

She stopped, breathless, looking from one of us to the other, her thin face desperate.

I didn't look at Jennifer. I couldn't.

"Rusty says he doesn't know anything about a box of papers. Felice says that's a lie, because she heard him tell Phyllis she had to return them at once. Phyllis said oh all right, if that was the way he felt about it, she would. Then she told Felice she wouldn't give them up for all the rice in South Carolina."

Anne Lattimer bit her lip until it was white. Jennifer sat there, tense and silent.

"Look, Jennifer." Anne's voice was pleading . . . and that too was a kind of tragic irony—her pleading with the child grown up that she'd hurt so desperately so long ago. "Will you see Colleton, and tell him I'm sorry, I didn't mean any of the things I said? I was angry, and hurt. Ask him to come and see me—will you?"

"If I see him I will," Jennifer said shortly. "I'm going back to Strawberry Hill. We don't have a phone. Why don't you call him up now?"

"I'm afraid to, they're watching everything we do," Anne said wretchedly.

Jennifer's eyes kindled like dark sapphires under a light.

"Why should you be afraid?" she said sharply. "You and Colleton were together all evening, weren't you? Mr. Michener said so."

Anne's face went a little paler, and I shouldn't have thought it possible.

"Yes," she said desperately. "Yes, of course we were."

"Then don't act as if you weren't.—You'd better get your things, Diane, if you're sure you can stick it."

Anne had gone when I came back with my bag. Jennifer was sitting behind the wheel, her eyes wide, staring in front of her.

"Look, Diane—would you do something? Go in and phone to the house. If Colleton's there, tell him he ought to see Anne right away. If he's not, tell mother, and tell her it's important. Would you mind?"

"Not at all," I said. I hurried back inside and put in the call. A dusky voice answered.

"No, miss. Mist' Colleton ain' here. Miz' Reid she just gone out. Ain' nobody here, 'cept Mist' Abbott. He waitin' foh Miz' Reid t' come home his self."

I put down the phone, my hand trembling a little. Felice had done what all the rest of us had tacitly committed perjury to keep from doing. Trying to involve her dead mistress's husband, and to take her spite out on a country and people she didn't like, she had touched the Achilles heel of Strawberry Hill. How vulnerable it was the Reids themselves were the only ones who knew.

I went back to the car. "They aren't home, either of them," I said.

The quick alarm in her eyes startled me.

"What else?" she asked quietly.

"Mr. Abbott's there, waiting for your mother."

She reached over and opened the door. I got in.

"Well, I guess that's that," she said. "The sooner we get to Strawberry Hill the better. We'll go out Tradd Street. We might meet Doctor John . . . he'll give Colleton the message."

We turned into Meeting Street, with St. Michael's white steeple shining out beyond the rusty pillared portico of the South Carolina Society building. It's one of the world's glorious streets. I never enter it without thinking again that if it were all of Charleston it would still be worth going half round the globe to see, and to walk down in early spring . . . to know that men were once, and still are, civilized, and to smell the nostalgic air full of flowers and the pungent fragrance of roasting coffee.

After a block or so we stopped in front of one of the famous so-called "single" houses. A silver plate under the brass knocker said "John Norton M. D."

Jennifer hesitated. "You drive on a little," she said. "I'd just as soon he didn't know you were going out with me.

101

He'll pester the life out of you when you get back about how Aunt Caroline looks and feels. I'll just be a second."

I'd be glad, I thought, to tell him about Miss Caroline— we don't have many such faithful lovers where I come from —but I took the wheel and continued along the narrow street. In a minute or two she came back. As we turned into Cannon Street and out the causeway toward the Ashley River bridge, she said,

"It's funny, isn't it, the way people's loyalties get all mixed up?"

I nodded. The sun going down beyond the low fringe of trees beyond Folly filled the air with a kind of mauve translucence that makes Charleston at sunset different from any of the rest of the world that I've seen. On our right the low marshes glowed softly, mauve and yellow and green-gold, along the blue ribbon of the river. Jennifer's eyes were fixed on the streaming traffic.

"Sometimes I wonder what it is that makes people choose the way they do," she said. "Take Aunt Caroline, when it came to choosing between her family and Doctor John. And Anne and my brother."

"I don't suppose you've thought about Jennifer and Rusty," I said casually.

"I suppose they're really what I was thinking about."

"——How long have you two been in love with each other?" I asked. It was pretty brash, I suppose, but there it was.

"I've adored Rusty all my life," she said simply. "I don't know that he cares anything about me, really. He's never said so. Ever since they've lived at Darien he's helped me. I wanted to farm, and he helped me with that, and marketing, and he gave me a couple of heifers that weren't good enough for his herd . . . at least that's what he said. We were just . . . well, sort of neighbors, until one day last spring."

We were going through that lovely stretch of great live oaks that makes the river road a sudden enchanted spot, with the pale pink and silver light making the long delicate strands of moss as soft as fairy smoke.

"It was fun, and awfully top-level—you know? And then one day we were down looking at the old break in our marsh. I thought I'd like to plant some Carolina gold rice. I slipped on a soft spot, and he grabbed hold of me and got me on firm ground again. And . . ."

She shrugged her slim shoulders.

"Well, that quick it was all different. We both knew it. It was like . . . well——"

"I know, darling," I said.

"We didn't say anything. He quit coming over every day, and I began letting Brad take me to parties when I had to go.

I don't think any one ever knew it. I never knew whether Aunt Caroline guessed it. She never asked why Rusty didn't come to see her the way he used to, so maybe she did guess. He still came once a week or so, but when I was away mostly, or if I was at home he didn't stay long."

We crossed St. Swithin's Creek and the rustic bridge. She got out and went to unlock the gate. I saw her stop, and then bend down and pick up the padlock and chain. I drove in as she pushed the gate open. She closed it behind us and got back under the wheel.

"Somebody's broken the padlock," she said, her blue eyes troubled. She didn't say anything more until we got to the old weather-beaten portico with its blind windows and barricaded door, and the pedestal with the nymph's feet forever fast. The drive was empty.

"Let's go around," Jennifer said. "Rachel will get your bag."

Her face was still troubled, kindled with a guarded anxiety halfway between fear and anger.

She glanced up at the two great brick chimneys, and down at the grass underneath. It was trampled a little.

"We've had visitors," she said with a wry little smile. "A week ago I'd have said Yankee tourists."

I followed her through a high hedge of thorny cassinas tangled with jessamine. We turned in the gate into the garden. One of the colored women—the less ancient of the two— was sitting on the steps. She got up as we came.

"This is Mrs. Baker, Rachel," Jennifer said. "She's going to stay with me a few days.—And who's been here?"

"Mist' John an' th' gentlem'n used be married t' Miz' Lattimer," the old woman answered. "They was lookin' fo' th' foreign 'ooman. Nobody cain' find her no place. They say tell you they goin' bring 'nothah lock fo' th' gate."

Jennifer looked at me with a puzzled face. "That's funny," she said slowly. "What made them think she'd be here?"

The next instant I saw her lithe body go suddenly taut, her eyes fixed with a quick dismay past me on something across the lawn. I turned. It was Felice. She was peering over the white gate. She glanced behind her, back down the path toward the river; then she came in, almost running toward us. Her pointed sallow face was so naked that I felt a little shudder of consternation go through me. Craft and cupidity sharpened by a nagging fear were in her bright narrowed eyes and etched in the deep nervous lines from her nostrils to the corners of her mouth. There was something else too: a bitter loneliness that made her tragic but in some way even more terrifying.

16

She seemed scarcely aware of me. Her whole racked soul was concentrated on the dismayed girl beside me.

"Mademoiselle!"

Her voice was an urgent desperate sibilant.

"I need money. You will give it to me. I will not say what I know; I will go back to France.—Five hundred dollars is all I want, mademoiselle, to go back to France!"

She gripped her writhing hands together, her eyes suddenly scalded with tears.

Jennifer's face was pale. "I haven't got it, Felice," she said quickly. "I'd give it to you if I had it . . . oh, believe me, I would!"

The Frenchwoman recoiled like a terrible dark flame, her thin face working violently, her eyes blazing into Jennifer's.

"Mademoiselle . . . you do not understand! I will tell them everything! It was you who stole the letters! It is you he is in love with! It is you he comes to see! It is to save you —this house the miserable lie you tell, the secret you will not tell—that you have murdered Madame so she could not tell! I know it all, do you understand? I will tell it!"

Her voice had risen to an hysterical scream. *"I will tell——"*

"Stop it!"

A man's voice cut through that dreadful mad flow like the lash of a whip. Felice jerked her head back, staring wildly at the porch. Rusty Lattimer was standing there, his blue eyes as cold as steel. The next instant he was down the steps.

"Get out of here." He spoke very quietly, but they tell me a cobra doesn't make much noise either. "Quick. Do you hear?"

For a second the habit of obedience paralyzed her body and her tongue. Then she broke loose again.

"I will not go until you give me money! You do not dare let me tell them what I know!"

Her voice rose again into an hysterical laugh. She turned, malignant-eyed, her thin forefinger shooting out at Jennifer. "She is the one! She will suffer!"

Rusty's hands gripped her arms. She tore at him, kicking and screaming like a wild thing.

"Oh, give her the money, Rusty!" Jennifer cried passionately. "For pity's sake give it to her and let her go!"

Silence sharp as a knife cut the air. Felice stood motionless, her black hair streaming, her face a corroded mask except for those black fiery eyes. Rusty's hands dropped abruptly. He looked at Jennifer, his face still hard as a rock, his eyes baffled and stung with sudden doubt. I saw quick new hope flicker in Felice's eyes.

"I can't stand it, Rusty!" Jennifer whispered desperately. "Give it to her . . . let her go!"

A chill that I'd never hoped to feel in the bright sunlight crept through the garden. Suddenly a window upstairs in the old drawing room went up, as electric as a machine gun barrage. Miss Caroline's frail exquisite face under her snowy hair and little lace cap looked down through faded ancient eyes. I saw Jennifer's face go white, her hands fall limp to her sides. Rusty was staring up, completely dumbfounded.

Miss Caroline's old voice, tremulous as a dying woodwind, touched us.

"Is something wrong, Jennifer? I thought I heard some one speaking."

Under the soft reedy notes came Felice's whisper, like a harsh, defiant and abruptly triumphant obligato: "I will tell her your lie!" . . . and Jennifer's frantic poignant "Oh, Rusty, please, *please!* For her sake!"

Then Rusty's voice, raised so that she could hear it.

"It's just us, Miss Caroline. Everything's all right."

He looked around at Felice and nodded. A smile of cool satisfaction moved her thin lips.

"Let Rachel close the window—you'll catch cold," Jennifer said.

Miss Caroline raised her porcelain face to the soft air, opened her half-blind eyes and smiled. Then the tiny black mummified figure that I'd seen picking up the potatoes in the desecrated room appeared beside her, and Miss Caroline moved away.

The four of us stood there for a moment, motionless and silent, Felice's sharp eyes glancing from Jennifer to Rusty and up to the empty window. If she'd shouted them out loud I couldn't have heard more clearly the words going through her tidy calculating mind . . . "This is their weakness, his because it's hers" . . . or known more definitely what she was thinking if she'd turned to Rusty and said, "This is worth more than a few hundred dollars to you, Mr. Lattimer." It was all written so plainly in the little cat's smile at one corner of her mouth.

"I will go now, Mr. Lattimer," she said. "I will see you this evening. I was going in town to see Mr. John Michener, but now I will not have to go."

She turned and hurried along the path and out the gate without a backward glance.

"——I'm so sorry, Rusty!" Jennifer said brokenly.

He stood looking down at her, his hands resolutely at his sides. "It's blackmail, Jenny," he said quietly. "It's not good enough, honey. And it never ends."

He took a step toward her. In another instant she'd be in his arms, her crumpled little face that needed him so badly crushed against his. I turned discreetly and fished a cigarette out of my bag.

Just then the door opened. The tiny turbaned Negress tottered feebly out. Rusty and Jennifer, still a million miles from each other's arms—a step can be so amazingly long—turned.

"Ol' Miss say will you come up, Mis' Jenny," she said. "She say it ain' proper fo' you to receive a man fo' his wife's col' in her grave. An' it ain'."

It wasn't, I suppose. I saw the hot flush that colored Jennifer's cheek as she picked up her hat and ran up the steps into the house. I looked at Rusty.

"You'll have to wait a bit, old boy," I said.

He sat down on the steps, his big roughened hands clasped between his knees.

"I'm sorry," he said. "I've been with her so much, so long now, that nothing else seems to matter much."

He looked out across the lawn toward the blue river beyond the green-gold marsh.

"She saved my soul," he said after a moment. "I was getting just like Brad—drowning all the things I've always believed in in the bottom of a highball glass. We came back here last year. There she was, just a kid, hanging on by her teeth. Her mother trying to make her get rid of all this before it caught up with her.—Mrs. Reid, I mean."

"It looks as if it's done it," I said. "You don't think you can buy Felice off for five hundred dollars, do you?"

His jaw hardened. "It's a damned outrage," he said. "She——"

I interrupted him. "Rusty—do you know what this is all about? I mean who killed Phyllis, and why? It *can't* be just this! I mean after all, nobody takes anybody else's life just to keep an old lady from finding out the front room panelling's gone. It doesn't make sense!"

He shook his head.

"I don't know what the hell it's all about, Diane," he said evenly. "But I wouldn't tell you if I did."

"——Do you know if that *is* the reason somebody killed Phyllis?" I asked. "Or is it just—money?"

He didn't say anything for a few moments.

"If you mean me, Diane," he said then, "I might as well tell you I don't want Phyllis's money. I didn't marry her

106

for it. I married her because . . . well, she seemed to have the same ideas I had about a lot of things. She wanted to farm."

He laughed, a very mirthless and disillusioned laugh.

"Or that's what she made me think. Oh well, what the hell. It was my fault as well as hers. I didn't want it this way, God knows."

He got up abruptly.

"I'll push along. I'm glad you're here. I didn't know I was in love with Jennifer until I got to waking up at night and worrying about her over here by herself, with Miss Caroline and those two old crocks. I used to get up and come over and look around, just to make sure they were all right. That's one of the things Felice told Abbott. She wouldn't have any way of knowing I just looked around and went home again."

"I guess that's not the way the people Felice knows would do it," I said.

He nodded. "I'll cut her throat if she's not careful."

"Don't say that!" I protested sharply.

"I suppose I shouldn't. Well, tell little miss her tenant farmer's waiting for the moon to change. So long."

The gate closed behind him. I turned around. The tiny black mummy in the white turban was still standing there. It flashed across my mind that she and Rachel were the real guardians of Strawberry Hill, moving silently, aware of everything, watching, waiting. They were the sphynxes at the temple gates, guarding a frail old empress whose tomb had long been sacked.

I thought of what a friend in Charleston had told me. If you're lost in the woods, or your car gets stuck jungle-deep on a deserted plantation road, you only have to wait a minute. Suddenly a Negro will be standing in the road. You won't have seen him come or heard his feet, but there he stands, with eyes that never sleep, materialized out of the deep psychic sub-stratum that lies warm and weird and hidden over the Low Country . . . as mystical as the grey moss that shrouds the oaks, as tropical as the heavy perfume of the gardenias and the magnolia, as dangerous—when it is dangerous—as the cottonmouth slithering through the marsh.

"Little miss say to come upstairs," she said.

I picked up my bag, went through the damp hall with its four closed doors and the single Chippendale chair that Doctor John had returned to Strawberry Hill, the hollow voice of the dismantled rooms speaking under my footsteps, and went hurriedly up the stairs.

Jennifer came out of the drawing room to meet me, her face troubled. "Aunt Caroline looks so exhausted," she said.

"Then I won't go in."

107

"Oh yes, she insists on it. It wouldn't do not to."

"By the way," I said. "Rusty said to tell little miss that the tenant farmer's waiting for the moon to change."

She turned her head quickly. "Oh, Diane, he must hate me! I know it's horrible . . . but there isn't any other way, there isn't, *really!*"

"He doesn't hate you, darling, if that's any comfort," I said. "He's head over heels in love with you."

She batted the big tears out of her eyes.

"I know I'm being a fool . . . but Diane, I adore him! I couldn't bear for him not to——"

She shook her head like a small duckling out of its first pond, and tried to smile. "Let's go in, shall we?"

We stepped across the threshold of Miss Caroline's lonely world. The fragile old lady in the brocade chair by the fire turned her faded eyes toward me. She looked so compounded of thistledown that I was almost afraid to take the transparent hand she held out to me. It was like touching something that flesh and blood had only to touch to destroy.

"This is a great pleasure for both of us, my dear. We don't entertain as often as we should. I'm much too frail. Jennifer must put you in the Lafayette room. He stopped here one night on his return in 1825. My mother remembered being allowed to carry up his shaving water, and spilling it on the stairs. She was five at the time. Do sit down, my dear."

As I look back on it now, that evening was the strangest I've ever spent. It might have been 1850 in Antigua, so remote were we from all the world. Miss Caroline's tremulous woodwind voice moved on the surface of a sub-silence as profound as the tomb. Her small tales lapped the beginning of the century and receded delicately, never touching a year I'd known by a decade or Jennifer had known by two. I had to tell myself that somewhere Time still lived. We ate supper in front of the fire, on lovely old French china and old silver. The knives and forks were of an exquisite pattern I didn't know, but there were only two sets of them, Miss Caroline's and mine. Jennifer's were the kind you get at the five-and-ten, but Miss Caroline couldn't see that, of course.

When the clock on the mantel struck nine, and the last genealogy was done, Rachel came in with an ancient wheel chair. Old Miss Caroline rose, leaning on her cane.

"Good night, my dear. If you hear sounds, it will only be the Colonel's ghost. He rides up as he did a long time ago, just as his soldiers break the Naiad from her pedestal. He is always too late to save her."

I gulped. It was fanciful, I suppose, but it seemed to me that history was repeating itself. Rusty was motorized now

. . . but gallop up in whatever way he might, wasn't he again too late?

Jennifer took a candle and followed her aunt and Rachel out. I sat there for a long time. She came back at last and put the candle down on the table again.

"Don't worry about the Colonel," she said with a little smile. "Though some people think the Yankee officers *were* rats."

She sat down on the ottoman in front of the fire, staring down into the flames. Suddenly she said, "It isn't my fault that Colleton doesn't marry Anne. Everybody always thinks it is. It's his own. It's because he's about mother the way I am about Aunt Caroline. We can't leave them."

She got up abruptly and moved over to the window.

"It's a terrible thing to say, Diane, but sometimes I think maybe it wouldn't be so awful if it . . . if it all did come out. It would be horrible for a moment, like the hurricane . . . and then there'd be new paint and new roofs, and a new cross on St. Michael's . . . and people might forget. They've forgotten more than this in Charleston."

I sat there staring at her, the firelight on her lovely pointed face under her curly black hair, trying desperately to understand what she was talking about.

"I know I'm being crazy," she said abruptly. "I know nothing would ever make me tell. You know, when I was little and used to read about martyrs and people they put on the rack, it didn't seem extraordinary to me.—I used to think I'd have made a lovely martyr."

"I think you have, Jennifer, rather," I said.

She shook her head. "No, it was easy, because it never hurt my heart."

The little French clock struck ten. Jennifer got up. "I'll just see how Aunt Caroline is—then we can go to bed. Lafayette's bed's at Williamsburg. You won't mind, will you? —This one's just as uncomfortable."

She smiled, took the candle and crossed the room. I sat there, the long shadows creeping up and receding in the firelight, listening to the silence. Suddenly I started up. Jennifer came running across the hall, her face white, her eyes like great black pools.

"Diane—quick!" she cried. "Aunt Caroline's ill—take the car, quick! Go over to Darien and phone Doctor Bates. Tell him to come, quickly! Oh, hurry, Diane—the keys are downstairs."

She stood there struggling to keep back the tears that flooded her heart.

I don't know how I got down those stairs as quickly as I did. I dashed out to the car. The nymph's small feet sprang out white and cold as I switched on the lights. I rounded the forgotten drive into the oak avenue, the silver moss in the white glare of the headlights beckoning to me like lost ghostly fingers, the dark oaks closing behind me in a cavern of night. The avenue had never seemed so long, the moss so silent and full of movement.

Almost at the end of the avenue I thought of the gate, remembered with a wave of relief that the padlock was broken, and saw the open gate as my headlights reached it. I raced madly through and turned right across the semi-circular road to the avenue leading to Darien. And I put my foot on the brake sharply.

Ahead of me in the drive was a car, its headlights full in my face. It was not moving, and there was something on the white sandy road in front of it. I switched down my far lights and slowed. As I did a man got up from the road and stood, his arms semaphoring; and there was something else still lying by the side of the road. A long streamer of moss flapped across my windshield as I drew up. The man came running toward me, and in the bright headlights I recognized John Michener.

I opened the car door and started to get out. He waved me back.

"No, don't, for God's sake, Miss Diane!" he cried. "Drive on up and tell Abbott I've found her. She's not dead yet—tell him to get a doctor quick!"

I pulled the door shut, my hands numb and shaking. Mr. Michener ran back across the road, knelt down by the inert form there. In the glare of his lights then I could see the dark body on the white sand . . . and a white face, staring horribly. By it, pushed frantically to one side, was a great wad of moss, its tendrils still stretching out like a monstrous web to claim their victim. I turned my head, too ill to move or start the engine I had stalled. I had seen Death before at Darien. I knew that I'd seen it there again. I closed my eyes, trying to blot out Felice's terrible face, and the tendrils of the grey moss still crawling toward it.

17

Felice's dead face still moved horribly in front of me, caught in the slow weaving fingers of the moss dripping eerily through the sharp white plane of my headlights. Actually in front of me, beyond the on-moving nimbus of light, past the dark mystically alive tunnel of ancient oaks, I could see the bright white pillars of Darien. In the mirror over the windshield I could see the tail light of the car back there in the road, a lone red star of death, receding into nothing. I pressed my foot harder on the accelerator. The car leaped forward, frightened and alive, through the dark winding line of trees.

I'd forgotten Miss Caroline; I'd forgotten the girl sitting beside the great four poster, the empty rooms echoing a hollow litany of despair. All I could think of was Felice's awful face . . . and the grey tendrils of the moss by it. The avenue had never seemed so long or sinister before, the bright façade of Darien so far away. Then abruptly the last long streamer of moss beckoned and was gone. I rounded the broad circle to the lighted portico. There were no cars there. The house looked bright and deserted, with the air of a lighted room where no one has been all night.

I got out and hurried across the porch to the open door, stopped an instant and listened. I could hear the slow ominous tick, tock, tick, tock of the grandfather clock on the stairs, but no sound of human voices. I ran into the drawing room. It was empty too. The long windows to the terrace were open. Through them I could see the dark lawn and the shining ribbon of the water beyond the rice fields. I ran across the room and out.

There on the wide brick half-moon at the foot of the porch I saw Anne Lattimer and Mr. Abbott. He was saying:

"Then, as a matter of fact, Miss Lattimer, nobody really saw your brother . . . nobody except the French maid."

I stopped short, my heart a cold lump in the pit of my stomach.

"But you can't believe what she says," Anne cried. Her voice was high and sharply edged. "She hates my brother, I tell you!"

"All right, all right, Miss Lattimer. All I'm sayin' is, I wish he'd come back and explain a few things. It don't look so hot, neither of them being around, after the way she's been carryin' on today."

It seemed to me minutes and minutes before I could move. Then I called "Mr. Abbott!" and ran across the terrace. "Mr. Michener's found Felice. She's down in the avenue. He said to call a doctor and to come. She's been——"

Anne Lattimer's face, white and terrible in the pale night, wouldn't let me say the rest of it.

Mr. Abbott stared at me. "Good God!" he said, his voice hardly audible. In an instant he was across the terrace. In the door he turned. "Call Charleston!" he shouted. "Tell 'em to send Doctor Thomas!"

He ran on, and I ran toward the door. As I did I heard a sudden noise behind me, and turned to see Anne Lattimer

111

running toward the old brick kitchen at the southern wing of the house. As I took down the phone in the library, I heard the plantation bell ring out, more urgently than I'd ever heard a bell ring before. It shattered the silent night, sounding hollow and metallic through the lighted empty house, ringing out across the dark lawns, over the marshes, through the woods, calling Rusty.

I put down the phone and went back into the hall. The bell still clanged . . . frantically, hideously. I ran back through the drawing room onto the terrace.

"Stop it, Anne, stop it!"

I fairly screamed to try to make her hear me. I could see her, almost exhausted with terror, shrieking through the tongue of the old slave bell for her brother to come back. Then she dropped the rope; the clamor died slowly across the empty lawn. No one had come. There were only the two of us there. Out somewhere the dogs barked excitedly, and I could hear Phyllis's hounds baying their dismal hollow wail.

Anne staggered back across the lawn. "Oh, where is he, Diane?"

"I don't know," I said. "But you don't have to wake the——"

I stopped abruptly. She couldn't wake the dead.

She just stood staring at me out of those haggard unhappy eyes. I shook her arm violently. "Anne—stop it!" I said. "Where *is* everybody? Where are the servants?"

"They've all gone," she whispered. "They started this afternoon. Mark was the only one here at dinner . . . now he's gone. They all slipped away. They're afraid . . . that's what's so terrifying, Diane."

It was, of course. Negroes are very strange in the Low Country. Fear seeps deep in ghost-ridden cabins and creeps through fields and into the houses, and suddenly where there were colored faces there are none. They've slipped away into the shadows.

"It's Felice they were afraid of. Maybe they . . . knew something. They do know things . . ."

I nodded slowly.

Suddenly I felt her fingers grip my arm, her nails biting into it. I listened. I could hear a car coming on the other side of the house.

"They're not bringing her here!" Anne cried. "Oh, they can't!"

She stopped abruptly as Mr. Abbott's tall figure appeared in the doorway.

"Your brother hasn't showed up yet, Miss Lattimer?" he asked, rather grimly.

"No," she said. I could hardly hear her voice.

Mr. Abbott pushed his hat back on his head and stood

chewing the end of his mustache. "I don't know just what we ought to do, I declare I don't."

He went slowly back into the house, and we followed. Doctor Thomas, a grey-haired man in a dinner jacket, was there, standing in the hall outside the library door with John Michener. Beyond them I could see a still form lying under an old raincoat on the leather sofa.

The men stopped talking as Anne and I came into the hall, and Doctor Thomas looked at the clock on the stairs.

"If there's nothing more I can do, I'll get back," he said. He started for the door . . . and it wasn't till then that the whole reason for my being at Darien at all flashed back into my mind. Old Miss Caroline . . . and Jennifer watching desperately at her side, in the lonely house up the enchanted avenue.

"Doctor Thomas!" I called. He stopped and turned.

"Miss Caroline Reid is ill. I came over to phone for some one. Would you go to Strawberry Hill?"

I didn't think for minutes why it sounded so strange. But it certainly did. All three of the men and Anne Lattimer stared at me with bewildered surprise.

"—Why . . . yes, of course, if they'll let me in," the doctor said. "You're sure . . ."

"Jennifer sent me herself," I said.

He shrugged. "I just don't want to make a wild goose chase this time of night. All right. I'll hurry over there."

I looked at Mr. Michener, bewildered myself.

"She hasn't had a doctor for many years," he said. "—Or let any one in the house."

He turned to Anne. "When did Rusty go out?"

The kindliness in his voice when he spoke to me had disappeared abruptly.

"He and Felice were talking on the porch about half past nine," she answered. "—Maybe he's over at the barn. All the Negroes have left the place."

Mr. Michener shook his head. "I've phoned down. No answer."

Mr. Abbott stood chewing the end of his mustache for a moment. He put his hand in his pocket and took something out. I looked past John Michener at it. I could see it quite clearly. It was a torn piece of paper, badly crumpled, about three inches square as it was torn and of a very familiar color. Mr. Abbott stood looking at it for a moment, then held it out abruptly to Anne.

"Is that your brother's signature?" he asked quietly.

Her face went as pale as death. She had to moisten her lips before she could speak. "—Yes . . . it is."

"Do you know any reason he'd have to give Felice Marin a check for $5,000.00, Miss Lattimer?"

113

Mr. Michener and I took a step closer. Anne's fingers opened and closed on the edge of the table by her side.

"Phyllis . . . promised her money to go back to France on," she said shakily. "I . . . suppose that's——"

Her eyes widened suddenly. We all turned to follow her gaze. Rusty Lattimer was standing in the open door, looking at the torn piece of the bank check in Mr. Abbott's hand. I could see his signature on it, and the " 'ce Marin" above it, and the "$5,000.00" above that.

Rusty looked from it to Abbott, his grey eyes burning black and dangerous. "If you have any questions you want to ask, ask me—not my sister."

"That's what I've been plannin' on doin', Lattimer," Mr. Abbott said coolly. "Only you're pretty hard to find, ain't you? Didn't you hear that bell ringin'?"

"I heard it, but I was busy."

"What doing, Lattimer?"

"That's my business."

"It's ours too," Mr. Abbott said evenly. He pointed through the library door. The silent figure lying under the raincoat on the sofa had the profound motionlessness that only dead things have. Rusty's eyes were harder.

"I know about that," he said.

I heard the jar of the table against the wall as Anne Lattimer steadied herself.

Mr. Abbott's slow voice did not change.

"How did you know, Lattimer?"

"One of the Negroes forgot to take a bottle of gin he'd cached in the garage. He came back to get it, saw you all down in the road, and told me."

"Where'd you see him?"

"That's my business too."

The only sound in the house was the tortoise-slow tread of the grandfather clock, and the quick tinkling hare's feet of the little Sèvres clock in the drawing room.

Mr. Abbott's eyes moved from Rusty's hard lean face to the torn check.

"People don't give torn checks for $5,000.00 to servants and take 'em away again so quick as all this, Lattimer."

"I gave her the check," Rusty said quietly. "I don't get what you mean by taking it away again so quick, Abbott."

"Nobody else would be likely to take it, would they? Take it off a dead woman and tear it up . . . to save you the trouble of explainin' how a woman everybody knows was tryin' to blackmail you had that much money . . . and how she happened to be dead?"

Rusty spoke with that maddening evenness that hadn't changed the tone or color of his voice since he came in the door. "I guess you're right, Abbott."

114

"I figure you must have been a little nervous and dropped a piece of it, Lattimer. I found it wadded up, alongside the road, when we turned the car around. I like to missed it at that.—I guess it's up to you to do a little explainin', if you can."

Rusty nodded.

"I haven't seen Felice since half past nine, Abbott. She was alive then. I gave her the check. I didn't take it back again. That's all I've got to say."

Mr. Abbott looked down silently for a moment, and a little grimly, at the torn oblong of blue-green paper. He folded it carefully and put it in his pocket.

"It's murder I'm dealin' with," he said slowly. "I'll have to ask you to come to town tonight and think it over in the cooler, Lattimer."

I heard Anne's horrified gasp, saw John Michener's quick movement of protest.

"I'm ready any time you are," Rusty said. "Will you take Anne in with you, Mr. Michener? She can't stay here alone."

My eyes met Rusty's for a sharp instant as I was standing there, as stupidly as an old sheep in front of a motor car, and I caught his quick warning. I literally shook myself to snap out of the stunned bewilderment that had me rooted to the floor.

"Well, I . . . I guess I'll be going," I said. At least I think I must have said something of the sort. I know that a minute later I was out the door and in Jennifer's car and racing madly back down that awful avenue of Lazarus-pale moss and monstrous black limbs that seemed to move together in front of me, alive in the path of my headlights, and fall back in the dark silence, not quite touching me. I hardly noticed the tangled cavern that led to the desolate house on Strawberry Hill. I went slithering over the bumpy grassy road and turned in the forgotten drive. The doctor's car was gone; there was nothing there but the nymph's marble feet, forever fast on the marble pedestal, and the blind barred windows.

As I turned off the motor and the lights, the front door opened. Jennifer ran out on the porch, an electric torch in her hand. Behind her the hallway was dimly lit with a single coal-oil lamp on the table. I could see her face, as white as a new magnolia under her dark rumpled curls.

"Diane—what is it?" she whispered.

"It's Felice . . ."

She nodded. "Doctor Thomas told me that. But what——"

"Rusty, darling. They've arrested him."

She stood perfectly still.

"He wasn't about. He won't say where he was, or anything."

She didn't seem to hear me for a moment. She just stood

115

there, hardly even breathing, it seemed to me. Then she turned and went slowly into the house. I followed, our steps echoing against the empty walls. I closed the door and put up the bar. Jennifer looked around as I crossed the hall, and sat down in the ribband-back Chippendale chair that Doctor John had returned to her.

"He was here, Diane," she said. "He came to tell me he'd paid Felice, and she'd promised to go as soon as they'd let her. He stayed to help with Aunt Caroline. Then he . . . he left, because I didn't want the doctor to see him here."

18

It all seemed so crazy and useless, some way . . . or it did until I started to say so and looked down at the white young face in the lamplight. Then it didn't . . . or it didn't look quite so crazy, at any rate.

"It isn't right for anybody to suffer for what other people do," Jennifer said. Her voice and the meaning of it seemed almost disembodied in the lonely house, like echo murmuring a soft undertone when the sound had stopped.

I started to say, "Then why don't you do something about it?" but I didn't. I felt helpless. All the standards of reason and practically seemed suddenly so invalid, faced with the shadowy thing I didn't understand but that I knew held Jennifer and Rusty and all the rest of them in a grasp as real as any reality I'd ever known.

She picked up the lamp.

"Aunt Caroline is better. It was just shock. The doctor says she ought to be all right in a day or two."

She moved to the stairs. I followed her up in the fitful moving shadow of lamplight. At the top of the stairs she stopped.

"Go to bed, Diane. I've got to think. I've got to decide what to do."

She looked at me with a strange poignant little smile as I started away. "—Did I say something about choosing loyalties?" she whispered.

She was dressed and standing by the fireplace when I woke up next morning. It was one of those cold wretched drizzling days that ruin the tourist trade in the gardens and must have made the early settlers feel they were back in England again. She didn't smile or try to. She just waited until Rachel had put the old balcony tray on my lap and padded silently out. I poured a cup of coffee and tried not to think too much.

"Anne and Colleton have been out," she said. "What happened apparently was Felice made an appointment for nine o'clock in town with Mr. Michener. She told Mr. Abbott she was afraid some one would try to murder her. When she didn't come Mr. Michener called Abbott, and they came out to find her a little before ten. She wasn't at the house and the servants were all gone. They separated to try to find her, and John Michener had just done it a minute before you came."

I finished my coffee. "What about the rest?"

"Brad went to bed early. He was getting up at five to go dove shooting. Doctor John was playing bridge with friends at the Charleston Club."

She hesitated.

"Mother was at home, Colleton was working at his office."

She pushed her hair back from her forehead with an infinitely weary gesture, and smiled a faint tired smile.

"Aunt Caroline's indomitable. She's in the drawing room already. She says she's outlived all the doctors she's ever had."

When she'd gone I put down my grapefruit spoon, washed at the Staffordshire basin in the corner of the room and dressed. Then I crossed the quiet hall and opened the drawing-room door.

Miss Caroline's hold on life looked tenuous and insecure indeed. Her hand trembled as I took it in mine. It was cold and bloodless except for the blue-corded veins standing under the thin transparent skin covering her brittle delicate bones. She seemed almost infinitely old, a bit of spun glass that had withstood all time and change.

Her almost colorless eyes brightened as I sat down on the needlepoint ottoman at her knee. She put her hand out and touched my hair gently. "Your grandmother's hair was straight as a string," she said.

"Mine would be too, if I let it."

"Men have a great deal to be thankful for in the change of manners," Miss Caroline said. "Girls in my day weren't nearly so attractive as they're supposed to have been. I'm sure many more of them would have got husbands if they'd had curly hair and red lips. I can't quite approve of red fingernails, but I'm sure that's just a prejudice. And I think short skirts are not only charming, but very sensible."

She folded her hands quietly in her lap.

"I've always thought Jennifer's mother was very old-fashioned about a good many things, and perhaps not old-fashioned enough about others. However, I expect she'll go to heaven. They say of Charleston that if one goes to St.

117

Michael's, is presented at the St. Cecilia and lives below Broad Street, Paradise is a matter of course. I've never cared for St. Michael's. My father always went to St. Philip's, when we were in town."

"You'll probably get to heaven in spite of it," I said.

"I doubt it very much, my dear. Sometimes I think I've been a very wicked woman. I've followed too much the devices and desires of my own heart. Perhaps if I'd stayed in town after I was ill, Jennifer would have been more with young people. She wouldn't have been thrown so constantly, and in such intimate and romantic surroundings, with Rusty . . . and she would probably have fallen in love more suitably."

"—Oh, *dear!*" I thought. I glanced quickly at the open door, hoping Jennifer was well out of earshot of all this.

"Rusty told me yesterday that he loved her very deeply, and that if he was ever free from the apparently quite unwarrantable—as far as I can understand it—suspicion that has fallen on him in connection with that unfortunate woman's death, he wishes to be allowed to address her."

It was a quaint way of putting it, considering how close to bloodshed he'd been a moment or so later. But the whole business was quaint however you looked at it—as quaint as it was tragic.

"I hope you gave him your blessing," I said.

"The Lattimers have always been very nice people," Miss Caroline remarked . . . so truly a Charlestonian that I'm sure an angel from St. Michael's must have heard and moved over to make room in heaven against her coming. "Except his grandfather's brother. He was quite disreputable, and was fortunately killed in a duel near Georgetown. His wife married a foreigner, but I always thought she was very pleasant. Although we never received her afterwards. She died of cholera in Rome. I'm sure cholera must be a very unpleasant disease."

"I think it must be," I said.

"I think death is horrible anyway," Miss Caroline said casually. "But quite interesting. I'm rather curious about it, myself. I've been waiting a good many years to see it walk in that door. But it's always somebody else. I think it must have been me it's been coming to the plantations for, and the others have got in the way."

I stared at her. I couldn't have been mistaken about those plurals . . . and she knew about Felice!

"First my nephew," she said. "Then that Northern woman."

I relaxed a little. It would have been too uncanny.

"I hope you will always be kind to Jennifer," she said, after a moment. "She will be comfortably off, of course, but

118

I think she should go abroad. My mother had gowns from Paris. I should like Jennifer to have them too."

"New York's better, now," I said.

"Then I'd like her to go to New York," Miss Caroline said composedly. "And now I think I had better rest a few moments. I hear Rachel coming. They're very severe with me."

She smiled a little wistfully, I thought, and let her small lace-capped head rest back against her chair. As she closed her eyes I looked up at the door. I know it sounds silly, but somehow I was relieved that it *was* Rachel I saw there. I'm not sure that if it had been Death I wouldn't have gone and stood in its way too, as the others had done. As it was Rachel I only got up and went out.

I knew very definitely that if I were Jennifer I'd regretfully, perhaps, but very firmly let Rusty or anybody else hang, or whatever it is they don't do to white men of property in South Carolina, before I'd disturb the pathetic fallacy on which the spider-silk thread of life in the faded musty drawing room behind me hung so tenuously. And oddly enough Jennifer's own words echoed in my ears: "Rusty'd understand." It might be a little difficult as they fastened the last strap around his ankle, but men had died in the Low Country before to save the same ideas differently stated, and the same women in the same secluded drawing rooms. Brad wouldn't have done it, my brother the publisher would have said frankly, "Nuts." Rusty would take it, the way his grandfather and uncle in Georgetown had taken it, let cholera strike where it would. And while I knew it was wrong and irrational, it wouldn't be the first or the last time men would die for less.

I crossed the hall. As I reached the head of the stairs Jennifer came up. She stopped on the landing and looked up at me. A quick tender smile warmed her sapphire eyes and wavered mistily, which was perhaps a trick of my own blurred vision.

"Miss Caroline's resting," I said.

She nodded, turned and stood there a moment, her eyes fixed out of the window toward the river. Then she looked back at me.

"I'm going in to Charleston," she said. "Will you come?"

My heart sank a little. I went down the stairs. We stood there looking out over the flower-bordered walks and neatly clipped green lawn, down the terraces to the river marsh, all grey and mauve and dull sienna under the damp leaden sky.

"It isn't right," she said softly. "I can't let it be . . . this way. I've been thinking about it. It isn't because it's Rusty. It's because it's Rusty that I thought I could let it be—because I've got so I think of him as . . . part of myself. I

119

suddenly thought just now, what if it had been Mark, or one of the other colored people over there. I wouldn't have let one of them suffer to save . . . one of us. Not even Aunt Caroline—and she wouldn't want me to."

She spoke very slowly. Her low voice vibrated softly through the hollow house.

"I hadn't thought of it that way before, just because it was so mixed up with him that I was willing to let him do what I'd do myself. But it isn't that way. It isn't right to let other people go on sacrificing themselves for you, no matter what the consequences are. Is it?"

"I'm afraid it's not," I said, not positively, because I wasn't positive about anything just then.

"They'll all think it's because I love him, and want to marry him, now that she's dead. But I shan't be able to marry him now, ever . . ." Her voice faltered. "—And when I'm as old as Aunt Caroline, they'll see they were wrong. They're wrong about so many things."

The dead hands of tradition dripping cobwebs like Spanish moss seemed suddenly to have entangled us. I realized with a little shock that "they" meant not her own family, but that hallowed landspit that lay below Broad Street on to the Battery, bounded by the Ashley and the Cooper till they flowed together to form the Atlantic and the Universe.

"My God," I said, "—don't be a total idiot! Why does what 'they' think mean so much to you? Are you going to be another Miss Caroline, and Doctor John, and your mother and John Michener, and live and die alone, just because of what people say?"

"Not exactly either," she said quietly. "You see, Diane, you just don't understand."

"I certainly don't," I said heatedly. "You might just as well go crawl in the tomb out there and close the door as make your own heart into one. Look at Charleston! Some one always says about every other woman you meet, 'My dear, she never married, because her father, or her brother, or her mother . . .' It's cruel and stupid, and it's——"

"I know." She interrupted me quietly. "Lots of things are stupid and cruel, but you have to do them. And you can't always judge people so easily. People have to act the way they're taught to act. The ones I've seen that have acted differently don't seem to me to be nearly as happy as the ones that haven't. Their lives may seem barren and empty to us, but the ghosts they live with are at least honest ghosts. And when you die they'll let you rest. They won't gnaw at you all eternity."

"Well, I guess I'm a child of darkness," I said helplessly.

"I'm afraid you are," Jennifer said, with a twisted smile.

120

"That's all that keeps us going . . . us and the Brahmins. Will you come along with me?"

"If you'll let an untouchable in your car."

Her face lighted with that quick transforming smile.

"*All* life's a compromise, they tell me. Anyway, you're all right. Didn't your grandmother come out at a St. Cecilia?"

19

It was curious how the whole aspect of the world had changed as Jennifer and I drove down the wet root-ridged lane under the live oaks. The fairy silver and pale mauve and white arabesque of light and moss and flowers had disappeared. The moss, funereal, stained black and green, liquid as pitch and as sinister, dripped heavily from the great leprous-lichened branches of the old trees, and hung like wisps of hag's-hair from the vines. The magnolia leaves shone glossy as patent leather, the wisteria sagged pale and purple. The gusty wind disturbed the moss till it foamed and writhed like the crests of a storm-driven sea.

We went through the open gate at the end. Jennifer slowed down, but she didn't stop and go back even to close it. In a sense, I supposed, it was the first step of her renunciation. Or maybe it was only because the people she feared most were gone now, and no tourist would venture to trespass up that black enchanted lane on a day like this.

I glanced up the other avenue of oaks. The moss hung there like a pall in the momentary calm. There was no sign where Felice had lain, out of sight of the moving fingers of light as Mr. Abbott's car crawled up the sandy road toward Darien.

Jennifer's foot went taut on the accelerator, we leaped forward across the narrow bridge and out the double line of magnolias to the road. Neither of us had spoken since we'd left the house. Neither of us spoke now as we crossed St. Swithin's Creek and sped along the wet highway toward Charleston. Jennifer's gaze was intent upon the road. Only her pale set face and eyes bluer than the indigo that had made the Low Country rich long before rice had come from Madagascar betrayed the struggle she'd waged and won. —Or lost? I didn't know. I didn't know how one could ever determine the outcome of such a struggle in terms of victory or defeat. Though a man lose the whole world and find his own soul . . . it kept going through my mind.

Just offhand, however, I think I'd rather she'd got Rusty and let her soul take care of itself. But Rusty, of course, had become both the price and the stakes, so that she seemed to me to be the loser whichever she did. Not that what I thought mattered at all. One sidelong glance at her taut erect little figure at the wheel, and her chin, and her eyes straight ahead of her on the road, made it evident that nothing would make her do any differently, no matter what the price or what the stakes.

We crossed the Ashley and swerved right across the asphalt lane between the palmettoes. The wind buffeted the light car as it bounced across the holes, splashing muddy water against the windows. One pleasant thing about such weather, I thought, was that the Citadel didn't stand out so glaringly on the landscape. We turned into Ashley Avenue, past the Rutledge Pond, and on to the Battery. The wind lashed the waves high over the sea wall, spraying the mud and bits of moss from the hood.

"You see, Diane," Jennifer said suddenly, "it isn't right to let any one suffer for something he didn't do."

"You sound like a phonograph record that's got stuck on one line, precious," I said, and was sorry the instant I did. She was definitely without humor just then.

"I suppose I do, but it's true anyway," she said calmly. "That's the reason I never want Aunt Caroline to know about Darien, or the rest of Strawberry Hill. It wasn't her fault that the gods she lived by grew old and died before she did. If faith can make them still seem to live, it's as good a religion as many other ones. It wasn't her fault my father was profligate and . . . ill-advised, or that my mother put off facing the music until it was too late to face it without destroying everything."

"Then if you make . . . everybody face it now, won't you destroy everything too?" I asked.

She didn't say anything for a moment. Then she said, "I probably will. But it's the old phonograph record again. It isn't right to make other people suffer to save yourself. In a sense Aunt Caroline is myself. I mean, Strawberry Hill and all the dream world it stands for mean more to me than to anybody else—even Aunt Caroline. If it goes to pieces it would kill her, I know—but she has courage to face death . . . more than I have to . . . to go on living, or mother has to face the disgrace that will come."

"Then can't you *wait?*" I said. "Maybe it won't——"

"That's what I can't do, Diane. As long as it was only us, that was one thing. But it's different now, don't you see? Even Phyllis didn't matter, because Phyllis had it coming to her. I know it's a dreadful thing to say, but she had. She was trying to destroy us, and we had a right to save ourselves.

But Felice is different. That's just murder.—I know she was blackmailing everybody, and it never would have ended this side of the grave, but I think the fact that she *knew,* so she could blackmail us, was a kind of . . . of punishment. All of it's that, really. It can't go on—it can't! Don't you see? It can't jeopardize the lives of people it doesn't concern, like Felice, or any one else who happens to stumble by. Or Rusty."

"But they haven't convicted him, Jennifer," I protested.

"Even if they haven't, suspicion does such *horrible* things to people. Knowing you're innocent, yet knowing every room you go into some one's thinking 'He was lucky to have got off,' or every street you walk along some old friend's nudging a tourist and saying, 'Don't look now, but that man killed his wife and her maid so he could get his wife's property and marry the girl next door.' You don't live as intimately with people as we do down here. You just don't know what that kind of thing can do to decent people."

We'd drawn up in front of the single house in Landgrave Street, gleaming white and freshly painted after the hurricane.

"I hope mother's home," Jennifer said, looking unhappily up at the windows. "I've got to see her . . . first."

My heart sank a little—She looked so like a young Jeanne d'Arc just then.

Through the old wrought-iron gate along the garden path I saw a colored man in a blue apron sweeping a rug on the long side piazza. The dust rose up in a pale cloud around the early white rose blooming on the trellis by the steps. It seemed curiously symbolic, some way, of all the past and of Jennifer.

The man touched his forehead and bowed. "Mo'nin', Miss. How's Miss Caroline this mo'nin'?"

"She's better this morning, thanks, Boston. How are you?"

"Po'ly, miss, thank you. You lookin' mighty peaked yo'self, Miss Jenny."

Jennifer smiled. "Is mother home?"

"Yes, miss. They all upstairs. Yo' ma, Mr. Colleton, Doctor John, Miss Anne, an' that No'th'n gentleman. Ah fo'gets his name."

"Mr. Porter?"

Jennifer's voice was startled and incredulous. She stood hesitating, just on the threshold of her mother's house, all the resolution she'd gained during that vigil by the fire at Strawberry Hill drained out of her. It was hard for me to understand. Why had Brad's being there changed it all so much? Was it because he was a foreigner? I was one too. The fact that my grandmother had been presented at a St. Cecilia couldn't, I felt, make this much difference.

Then it occurred to me that maybe it wasn't Brad. Maybe it was all the rest of them, since it was her mother she'd come to see. It was so incongruous, some way, this struggle going on. I looked at Jennifer in her blue checked jacket and dark blue skirt and little blue riding hat with a parrot's feather in the band. It was drama here that ought to be more suitably clothed, and in a more tragic setting than an open front door of a Charleston house with an old darkey sweeping the dust out of a worn rug on the piazza. For it was tragic drama . . . the conflict of love and duty, of old dead gods and new golden ones, of a world of reality and a world of dreams.

She went slowly inside. The house was chilly and very silent. The doors on either side of the transverse hall were closed. Jennifer put her bag and car keys on the table under a rather cheap modern mirror and stood there, her hands touching the pink petals of the azaleas in the white bowl on the table. Suddenly she dropped them at her sides.

"I can't, Diane, I can't!" she whispered. She closed her eyes. "I just can't, that's all!"

"Don't, then, Jennifer," I said.

She stood a moment looking around the shabby hall. "Let's go up," she said wearily.

I followed her up the stairs. There were two closed doors here too. From the one on our left as we rounded the turn in the stairway I could hear Doctor John's high-pitched, rather querulous voice saying, "Rusty was a fool to have paid her anything. Blackmail has an ugly sound."

Jennifer's hand on the bannister went taut, her slim body stiffened.

Anne Lattimer's voice edged with anger came through the closed ill-fitting door. "—Rusty wasn't paying blackmail. He was just giving her the money Phyllis had promised her so she could go back to France."

"Nobody's likely to believe that." It was Brad's Northern voice, and certainly a Northern sentiment. They may be realists in the South but they don't speak out in drawing rooms.

Mrs. Reid's gentle reproof was barely audible. "I'm sure Rusty was only being kind to the poor woman, Bradley."

"Yeah?" Brad Porter said curtly. "Then why didn't he give it to her before she started raising hell all over town? It would have saved everybody a lot of headache. Abbott may be a country cop, but Michener's nobody's fool. Neither was Felice.—And not to inject a sour note, but one of your local bank presidents was saying at lunch yesterday that his old friend Doctor John must be getting ready to cash in —he'd drawn out $2500. The biggest check he'd ever written before was $167 for income tax."

124

There was a silence so sharp that the damp air seemed to freeze.

Doctor John's high treble fairly sizzled. "You'll mind your manners, young man. A man still has a right to do as he likes with his money."

"Okay," Brad retorted. "I didn't say he hadn't. I'm merely saying that this town's a sieve, and that when somebody sees Colleton leaving your house looking like he'd been in a train wreck, and you dash out two minutes later and draw twenty-five hundred bucks out of the bank, and a woman's murdered because she's blackmailing a guy that's in love with the daughter of the house . . . well, it doesn't take long for the whole town to add it all up and get a pretty heavy score."

I looked at Jennifer standing there, her hand still gripping the banister, her body perfectly rigid, the hot color burning in her cheeks.

"I mean, it's okay with me, as long as they count me out," Brad said objectionably. "As for Rusty, you can hang him to the first tree if you like. You'll be doing me a favor."

Jennifer was across the hall like a flash. She threw open the door, her eyes blazing.

"Nobody's hanging Rusty!"

Her voice was hot with passionate denial.

"That's why I came, to tell you all that . . . you, Mother, and you, Colleton, and Anne . . . all of you! I know who killed Phyllis, and it wasn't Rusty! And I know why she was killed, and it has nothing to do with him! He shan't suffer for it, I'll not let him!"

The five people in the room sat or stood utterly dumbfounded, like sudden pillars of salt. Mrs. Reid and Anne on the sofa in front of the coal fire, Brad, his elbow on the mantel, galvanized out of his nonchalance, Colleton by the garden window, Doctor John stiff and erect as some ridiculous weathervane in a straight chair facing the sofa . . . and all of them—it raced absurdly through my head—like a party in a parlor, all silent and all damned.

Mrs. Reid, her lips white, her blue eyes appalled, was the first to recover. *"Jennifer!"* she cried.

"I know, Mother," Jennifer flashed back hotly. "That's why I came. I wanted you to know before I did it. I thought I could make you understand . . . but I can't, you're all too smug and satisfied that it's the business of somebody else to bear the burdens you're too cowardly to bear yourself! It's all right for us, but Rusty shan't have his life ruined. I'm going to Mr. Michener *now,* and I'm going to tell him *everything!"*

And she was out into the hall and running down the stairs. I hardly saw her go. All I was aware of—and that quite uncomprehendingly—was Mrs. Reid's horror-stricken face and

125

her hand moving desperately toward her throat, and Anne's voice: "Colleton! Stop her! Stop her!" . . . and Mrs. Reid's weaving body pitching forward in a silent heap on the floor.

Doctor John sprang forward, Colleton, half-way across the room, wheeled sharply. In an instant he was on his knees beside his mother. Anne, her face haggard, sat motionless in the corner of the sofa as if that one unheeded cry was the last effort she could ever make. I glanced at Brad. He was looking at me with an almost calculating and certainly pretty smooth eye. I felt my face flush—I don't know why. I do know that then and there, as I shifted my gaze to the four people around the sofa, something happened inside me. I don't even now know what it was . . . I only know that I had a strange feeling that Jennifer needed some one now worse than she ever had in that strange little life of hers.

Colleton Reid, his eyes dark with anger, his lips compressed to thin steel, lifted his mother to the sofa. I knew Brad was still watching me. Out of the corner of my eye I saw him move a little. I got to the door first and out. I heard him coming after me down the steps. I couldn't very well break into a dead run, and anyway it wouldn't have done me much good if I had, I knew that. So I slowed down until he caught up with me at the wrought-iron gate in the garden wall.

"There's no use dashing about like a fire engine, lady," he said composedly. "John Michener phoned in a few minutes ago. He won't be back from Darien for another hour anyway."

My heart, already in the pit of my stomach, sank another notch.

"Then there's all the more reason for me to hurry," I said. I quickened my pace. He quickened his.

"The little gal sure threw a stink bomb in the bosom of that family, didn't she?" he asked sardonically.

"If that's what you call it," I said.

"I can't think of anything else just offhand."

We turned out of Landgrave Street and got to Meeting Street.

"Look, Diane—will you tell me one thing . . . honestly?"

"Maybe," I said.

"Does old Miss Caroline exist?"

I stopped dead in my wet tracks and stared at him.

"Of course. Did you think she didn't?"

He laughed. "One way of getting the truth out of a woman is to surprise it out of her. I've been wondering. You know, I think Phyllis had the notion originally that she didn't."

126

"That's nonsense," I retorted. "Phyllis saw her, and spoke to her. Didn't she tell you?"

He shook his head.

"Well, something's screwy out there—what is it?"

"I wouldn't know," I said.

"Phyllis knew."

"—And told Felice," I added.

"And another redskin bit the dust," he added too, sardonically. "It's funny how they're bleating about blackmail now. If Phyl wasn't trying to blackmail the whole gang, I miss my guess."

"It has an ugly sound, dear," I remarked.

"And an ugly look," Brad said. "Look here, Diane."

He stopped. The street was empty except for an old colored man with a pushcart.

"—What the hell was Phyllis after in that house? Don't tell me antiques, because I know as well as you do that Phyl had about as much interest in antiques as an alley cat."

"It was antiques, at first," I said. "She wanted them, and Strawberry Hill too, just because she couldn't get them. The rest of it was something else again. You know almost as much about it as I do. Which is precisely nothing. All I know is that Mrs. Reid wanted her to have Strawberry Hill, to get Miss Caroline and Jennifer out and wipe out a lot of old scores. She seems to have brought all this on herself instead."

Brad didn't say anything. So I said, "Now will you tell me something . . . honestly?"

"Probably not, but go on."

"Did Phyllis actually tell you she was going to marry you again?"

He didn't answer at once. I looked up at him. His tanned, handsome but definitely too indulged face had a slightly grim and rather sardonic expression.

"She did tell me so . . . honestly."

"Then why did you get blotto that afternoon?"

"Because I was still pretty fond of her . . . and I knew she was lying. To put it in the Northern way, I knew she was just rigging me to get me to do something she wanted done."

"What was it?" I demanded.

"I didn't make it out, entirely," Brad said. "It smelled from the beginning and I wasn't having any. I told her so. Phyl could be a first-rate rattlesnake when she put her mind to it. I thought it had something to do with the old lady. That's why I wondered if she actually is out there."

"She's very much there," I said. "And she's sweet—all wadded up in cotton wool. And I hope she stays that way till she dies. Jennifer thought she was dead last night, but this morning she's fine again. She'll probably outlive us all."

127

We'd reached St. Michael's and were standing by the door. Across the street a few colored women with their rain-soaked blossoms and magnolia leaves held the fort in spite of wind and weather.

"I've got to go," I said. "Lord, Brad, I wish none of this had ever happened! Why *did* Phyllis have to be such a fool!"

His eyes, fixed across the street, had a grim kind of despair in them that I'd never have thought him capable of feeling.

"It's Felice I feel sorry for, somehow," he said shortly. "Phyl always gambled, and she always used other people for chips. Felice was one of them. Maybe if Phyl had played a straight game . . . Oh, well, what the hell.—There's only one thing I'd bet my own money on.

"It must be pretty safe then," I said. "What is it?"

"That that twenty-five hundred the old codger drew out was for Colleton to buy off Felice with."

I followed his glance across the street. Doctor John's absurd brown Panama hat was bobbing up and down in the little crowd crossing to the other side of Broad Street on the green light.

I started away.

"Well, so long," Brad said. "I'll be seeing you."

20

Just then a woman coming out of St. Michael's grabbed my arm. "My *dear!* I'm *so* glad to see you! Have you been to the exhibit at St. Philip's? My dear, it's simply enchanting. How long will you be here? You must come in this afternoon for tea!"

Her face was vaguely familiar, but who she was or where I'd met her I hadn't an idea and still haven't. I only know that by the time I'd got loose Doctor John had disappeared. I dashed in front of a car making a right turn on a red light, heard a Southern gentleman swear at a Northern lady, and went as quickly as I could without actually running to the Court House corner and across Meeting Street, still against the red light, my heart pounding.

What I thought might happen to Jennifer I don't know, but it's unknown fears that are the most awful. The idea that she might be sitting alone in Mr. Michener's office, waiting for him to come back from Darien, and that some one might come in and silence forever the last tongue that could speak against him racked in my brain. I hurried past the building on the corner and turned into the narrow court behind it. No one was in it, except a colored boy in a white coat—no one that I knew. I ran across the cobbles and up the steps into a narrow hall plastered with rusty sign plates. I turned and looked back out of the door.

Doctor John was at the entrance of the court, talking to a colored woman. I opened the door that had "John Michener, Counsellor-at-law" in black frayed letters on it and closed it quickly behind me. The outer office was empty. I could hear the murmur of voices from the inner office, and saw Jennifer's head outlined against the frosted glass.

I drew a long breath of relief . . . from what I'm not sure—just relief. Nevertheless I reached out and slipped the catch on the patent lock. Then I went and sat down by the desk and waited. It was like waiting for doom, in one way, and doom isn't so easy to wait for. I took out my vanity and powdered my nose, and repaired my motheaten lipstick. It's as good a way as any to wait for it, I suppose. I tried to think, then I tried not to. It all seemed so tragic and unnecessary. One spoiled predatory woman had brought so much down on so many heads.

I put my impedimenta back in my bag and closed it. As I did I heard a quiet step in the outer hall. I looked up, my fingers suddenly trembling. I saw a large dark blur through the glass and the knob turned, slowly. I picked up the phone on the desk and pressed a button beside it.

Mr. Michener's voice answered, "Yes?"

"This is Diane Baker," I said. "There's somebody at the office door. I locked it. Shall I let them in?"

"Certainly."

His voice sounded a little surprised, and I felt like a fool. What, I thought, if Jennifer, for instance, had changed her mind and not told him at all? I would have made both of us look pretty silly.

I put down the phone, unlocked the door, opened it, and gasped. It was Rusty.

"—Where's Jennifer, Diane?" he asked curtly. "Doctor John said she was here?"

His eyes were so extraordinarily charged with something —consternation, despair, Heaven only knew what, exactly, and his voice so desperately urgent, that I couldn't speak. I could only point to the inner door.

He caught his breath sharply and took a quick step forward. Halfway across the room he stopped. The office door opened. Jennifer, her face streaked with tears, came out. She stopped dead, her mouth open, her eyes suddenly wild with dismay.

"Rusty!" she cried. *"Oh——"*

At that instant I saw the tall figure of Mr. Abbott in the

door. He looked from one of them to the other . . . at Jennifer staring at Rusty and Rusty there staring back at her.

I suppose he meant to be kind. He said, "The charge against Mr. Lattimer has been dropped, Miss Reid."

Jennifer's face crumpled. *"How awful!"* she whispered. "I——"

And at that moment a deafening crash like a million bricks smashing down cut off the rest of that horrified whisper. We all stood there motionless for an instant; then Rusty and Mr. Abbott sprang to the door of the inner office. Abbott wrenched it open, took one stride forward and stopped dead. Jennifer reeled against the desk, her eyes closed, her face like chalk. I sprang after Mr. Abbott, and stopped too.

John Michener was sitting bolt upright at his desk, a thin oozing trickle of blood seeping out of the blackened hole in his forehead, the gun in his hand fallen, sprawling on the ink well in front of him. The pungent acrid smell of cordite filled the room like a pall of terrible incense. I leaned, half-blind with sudden nausea, against the door frame. Mr. Abbott moved heavily across the narrow space to the desk, laid his fingers for an instant on John Michener's wrist, and stood there, looking down at him. Then he leaned forward and picked up a sheet of paper on the desk pad. The words as he read it came blurred to my ears.

"To the Police of Charleston County:—I hereby state and affirm that I did with my own hand, on the 13th day of March, take the life of Phyllis M. Lattimer, and that on the 15th day of March, I did, in the same manner, take the life of Felice Marin; that I am alone responsible for their deaths; and that my reasons for taking their lives were entirely personal and private, and in no way concern any other person now living. I wish to state also that in a last emergency, I should not have allowed any other person to be convicted of their deaths.

"John Legare Michener."

I turned my head away. Jennifer had come slowly to the door and was standing there, her head held erect with extraordinary effort, looking at Mr. Abbott, avoiding Rusty's eyes. Mr. Abbott folded the paper with slow fingers, put it in his pocket and looked down at the desk again. A sealed envelope was lying there. I could see, and I knew Jennifer could see, scrawled in thick black letters, as if the ink like his own life-stream was running low, the words "Mrs. Atwell Reid."

As Mr. Abbott's hand moved down to pick it up, Jennifer sprang forward and snatched it from under his fingers.

"That's my mother's!" she said quietly.

Mr. Abbott's jaw tightened. It was a reflex, I suppose, more than anything else, because it relaxed again. He looked silently at her for a moment, and nodded.

"Take it to her, then, Miss Reid," he said, almost gently.

In the door Jennifer swayed a little, and Rusty sprang to her side. He caught her arms and held her, looking down in her bloodless face. Her head drooped forward, her hair touching his shoulder for a brief instant. She raised it again.

"Better let her sit down a minute," Mr. Abbott said.

She sank into the chair he pushed forward, her eyes closed, her hand gripped tight in Rusty's.

"—Don't feel bad about it, Miss Reid," Abbott said in his slow drawl. "I figured it was this way. I was just comin' to tell Mr. Michener so. There wasn't any other way to figure it, after last night. If the French woman had been in the road we'd have seen her. I wouldn't have been sure, though, if Mrs. Baker hadn't come along like she did. I guess you were almost an eyewitness, Mrs. Baker."

I stared at him, suddenly quite sick, as the whole awful business flashed back to me . . . the dark figure on the road, the semaphoring arms, the moss torn from her face as he'd seen my light.

"Anyhow, you'd have been bound to see anybody leavin' if there'd been anybody to leave," Mr. Abbott said. "Mr. Michener said she was supposed to meet him at ten, and I guess he was tellin' the truth all right."

"But what for, in God's name!" Rusty said harshly.

Mr. Abbott looked down at the written confession he'd taken from his pocket. "—For personal and private reasons that don't concern anybody now living," he said dryly. He turned to Jennifer. "I guess maybe somebody at your house could tell us, Miss Reid. The reason he killed the French woman is easy enough. She was upstairs when he went up and when he came down. I never told him I found a few threads of moss in his overcoat pocket the next day. I couldn't see any reason he'd have for killing Mrs. Lattimer, after all he said about her being a client of his."

He folded the paper and put it back in his pocket.

"You take Miss Reid back home, Mrs. Baker," he said. "Lattimer, you better stay here, I guess, for the looks of things. I'll phone your brother, Miss Reid."

I don't remember how we got out of that office into the court and over into Landgrave Street. I followed Jennifer—still clutching the envelope, the wet ink running blurred like dark moss around the pen strokes of her mother's name—inside and up the stairs. Mrs. Reid was standing by the back window, Colleton Reid beside her, his arm around her shoulders. As they turned, the two of them looked at the girl in front of me for an awful moment. I saw her stiffen, her pale face go a little paler, her head rise, her shoulders straighten like a young fern. None of them spoke.

Jennifer said then, "I'm sorry, Mother . . . there was nothing else I could do!"

Her voice must have sounded cool and heartless, I knew. They couldn't know all that had gone before.

She moved then, holding out the letter in her hand. "He wrote this to you."

Mrs. Reid looked at it dumbly for a moment. Colleton took the letter silently and put it in her hand. Mrs. Reid still stood motionless, a spasm of pain shooting through her face. She handed it back to her son. He took it, his face drawn and hard, opened the envelope, took out the letter and put it in his mother's hand. She moved unsteadily over to the chair by the fire and sat down, the pages trembling in her fingers. After a long time she let it fall into her lap and sat staring dry-eyed into the fire.

Jennifer's voice broke the silence.

"—There was nothing else I could do!"

It was low and passionate, and it vibrated across the still room like the cry of a small wounded animal in the wilderness.

"—There was nothing else you could do, Jennifer," Mrs. Reid said softly. And Jennifer turned and flew across the room, and threw her arms about her mother. "Oh, Mother, forgive me! I'm so sorry, so terribly, terribly sorry!"

She burst into a storm of heartbreaking sobs, her head buried in her mother's lap. Mrs. Reid bent down and kissed her dark hair.

"There was nothing else you could do, Jennifer."

Then Mrs. Reid raised her head sharply. Downstairs I heard the tread of feet. I saw Mrs. Reid's face contract again with despair. She closed her eyes for an instant; and then she made, I think, what must have seemed the last sacrifice. She snatched John Michener's final love letter from the floor where it had fallen and threw it into the blazing coals. The flames licked it, reared it up into a fiery mass and let it fall, black and curling, into nothing, as I moved aside in the doorway.

Mr. Abbott and little Doctor John walked in. Mrs. Reid had raised Jennifer to her feet and risen herself, perfectly controlled. Colleton came from the window and stood by her, his eyes wary.

"I'm sorry to trouble you, ma'am," Mr. Abbott said. "There's a few points I'd like to clear up, if you'll help me."

"I'm afraid there's nothing I can tell you," Mrs. Reid said quietly. "You said, I believe, that Mr. Michener had written a complete confession, and that no one else was involved. I don't see that it leaves anything to be added."

132

"There are one or two points, ma'am," Mr. Abbott said evenly. "I thought in his letter to you——"

"It was entirely personal, Mr. Abbott. And I have destroyed it."

She glanced at the grate. So did he. A thin film of grey still intact ash showed clearly that she had.

Mr. Abbott hesitated only one instant. "Then I guess it's all settled, ma'am," he said. I don't know whether I read the touch of irony into that myself, or whether it was there. "I'll bid you all good morning."

Colleton followed him to the door, and came back.

"I think that does in fact settle it," Doctor John said gently. "I am myself curious about one point, my dear. When Mrs. Lattimer went to John to see about a divorce . . ."

"She did not go to see him about a divorce," Mrs. Reid said slowly. "She never had the least intention of getting a divorce. She went to see him about another matter entirely. And Felice the maid knew it."

The pulse throbbing in her throat was the only sign of emotion in her. A Samurai child's training may be more severe, but it's no more effective than a Charleston lady's.

"John's only regret was that Rusty's check was found on Felice. He hadn't planned on that. He had arranged to meet her at the end of the avenue at ten o'clock. Mr. Abbott's coming upset his plans."

She stood, erect and quite lovely.

"I'm afraid I have very little sympathy for either of those women. My only regret is that John could find no other way. And now if all of you will leave me a few moments . . ."

Jennifer and Doctor John and I went out into the hall and closed the door. Jennifer took hold of my arm.

"Diane—I think I'll stay here all night with mother. Would it be too awful for you to go out to Strawberry Hill, and tell Aunt Caroline, and stay all night? And send for me if she isn't all right, won't you? Rachel and Martha never sleep, but I don't like to leave her alone with nobody there with a car."

"I'll be glad to," I said.

"If you wouldn't really mind——"

"Not in the least," I said.

She bent forward and kissed me suddenly on the cheek, just as Colleton came out. He looked at her silently for a moment, the resentment against her still burning in those deepset harassed eyes of his. Suddenly she made a little move nearer to him, and looked up into his face.

"I'm sorry, Colleton," she said softly. "I didn't want to be a traitor. I had to . . . I couldn't bear for Rusty to suffer like . . ."

133

His eyes searching hers softened. He put his hands on her shoulders and shook her a little.

"I understand, sis—I honestly do."

He bent down and kissed her forehead. There were tears in his eyes. "Now beat it. And don't be a little idiot. If you're staying with mother, I'll go out and see Anne."

Jennifer smiled suddenly.

"Maybe if you asked her to marry you, she would," she said.

"You mind your own business, brat," Colleton said. But he smiled.

I'd always assumed that the Greek catharsis Jennifer had spoken of meant pity and fear. For Colleton it had meant pity, certainly, but also hope.

21

I hardly noticed the Ashley River as I crossed it. John Michener's suicide and confession had cleared up a great deal, of course; it had also left a great deal not clear at all. It was like putting the last piece of an elaborate jigsaw puzzle in place, and looking down to find a large hole in the most important spot with nothing left to put in it. That he'd been in love once with Mrs. Reid I'd known from my mother's friend that night at the Dock Street Theatre. That he was still in love with her after so many years, I'd never have guessed. And even then . . . I tried to think back over the hectic days since that night in the walled court during the intermission. I'd never seen him look at her or speak to her except most formally. It seemed so extraordinary as to be fantastic that he'd never married her. It didn't make sense, not even in Charleston, where such very odd things seem to make the most extraordinary sense.

Then it struck me quite suddenly that this was true Charleston . . . the whole thing ending suddenly in silence. I thought of a lot of things I'd heard about from time to time. They all ended just that way. Some people knew and kept quiet. Some people guessed a lot of things and didn't keep quiet at all. But nobody knew, actually—nobody who talked. I could almost hear the tinkle and clatter and chatter of a hundred candle-lit tea tables, and a thousand busy tongues silencing instantly when one of the Reids or Micheners or Lattimers came in. It would go on forever. A Yankee tourist would come fifty years from now and somebody's great-grandchild would say, "See that old gentleman planting cabbages? That's old Mr. Lattimer. His wife and her French maid were murdered at Darien. Nobody ever knew the truth of it. One of the Micheners did it—nobody ever knew why."

It was fair enough, I suppose. After all, who was I to deny an old city one of its most cherished customs? Other Yankee tourists would wonder too, as they walked through paths of flaming azalea and touched and corroded with their touch the blush-pink camellias. Charleston's secrets would always be like the goblin shapes of a thousand cypress trees . . . just far enough above the black water to breathe and keep alive.

One thing I did know; and I'm not sure how I felt about it. Phyllis had lied when she said she'd seen John Michener about getting a divorce. I wondered suddenly. Had he himself been a party to the sale of Darien? Some one had executed the deed that old Miss Caroline, half-blind, had signed. I didn't know, of course, and I never would. Jennifer, I knew, would never speak of any of it again, and as far as the rest of the Reids were concerned, I knew the last word had been spoken when Mr. Abbott said, "Then I guess it's all settled, ma'am." Their subterfuge was safe again, old Miss Caroline would never know now how desperate the battle to save her enchanted hour had been.

I turned in at the iron gate and crossed the rustic bridge, stopping a moment to look up the two oak avenues—the well-kept one where death had walked, the old one overgrown with moss and flowers where death was waiting patiently and in peace till time should call. They were symbols, both of them; they had been from the day Phyllis Lattimer came to Darien. And they were something more, for the victory had gone to Strawberry Hill. Rags had stood against riches, a child guarding a frail moss-spun dream had stood against a worldly predatory woman and had won.

I turned up the old uneven lane. The sun struggling through the last rain clouds raised it all in a fairy canopy of silver and mauve, the white dogwood and glossy magnolia leaves painted an arabesque of light. In front of me the six slender columns of the weather-beaten portico stood like a temple entrance. The little marble feet on the pedestal seemed suddenly at rest, knowing the old blind house was safe again.

I got out of the car and went around to the garden gate. Rachel was smoking her pipe on the steps.

"Miss Jennifer is staying in town with her mother tonight," I said.

She got up, nodding her head. "Miss Jenny ain' never stayed away from home all night befo'," she said.

"I know."

"I 'spec' her ma takes Mist' John's death right hard," she said.

135

I didn't answer, or ask how she knew. By that curious grapevine, I supposed, that spreads like a vast intangible scuppernong, silent and more mysterious than the night.

"—Does Miss Caroline know?"

Rachel nodded. "I tol' her."

"How is she?"

"She's up. I cain' make her go to bed. She ha'd haided as th' debbil."

"Shall I go up?"

She nodded and opened the door for me, and I went into the dim damp hall with its simple cornice and the four closed doors with the strawberry leaves and flowers and fruit carved over them. And it was very strange. The house had lost all its eerie ghostliness for me. The hollow voices under my feet were friendly welcoming voices.

I went upstairs and opened the drawing room door. Miss Caroline, sitting in front of her fire, turned her dimly blind eyes.

"Diane?"

"Yes, Miss Caroline. Jennifer's staying in with her mother tonight."

The old lady nodded her snow white head with its tiny lace cap.

"I'm glad," she said. "Sit down, child."

I sat on the ottoman at her feet. She was as erect as a Dresden doll in a Dresden chair, her delicate hands folded in her lap. She seemed so old and frail I hardly dared to breathe for fear I'd blow her away.

She smiled at me.

"I wonder if I told you, Diane, that our Colonel—the one who rides up when we are in danger—was your great-grandfather?"

"No," I said. "You didn't."

"He'd been in love with my mother. That's how I came to know your grandmother and visit her at the No'th. He was an officer—it was many years later, of course—in the Union army. He kept his men from burning this house. They'd already broken down the little statue. My father would never allow them to raise it. It's still in the pond behind the quarters."

She sat looking at me a long time. Then she put out her hand and touched my hair gently.

"You've come to us instead of the Colonel this time, Diane. I've been very happy that you're here."

She hesitated.

"I want you to do something for me. I want you to listen to an old woman's folly, and keep it in your heart. Then I want you to take the papers in the leather box in the drawer, and burn them for me. Will you?"

"Yes, Miss Caroline, of course," I said. My voice wasn't very steady.

"I have been a very wicked old woman, Diane. Three dead faces haunt me from these shadows. I took their lives . . . not with my own hand but by my own bitter folly."

The little clock on the mantel ticked softly. Outside the evening light loomed silvery-gold up from the river marsh.

"Many years ago my nephew married a girl I didn't approve of. She was in love with John Michener. That was the reason I didn't approve . . . there was no other. I think she thought it would be easy to forget the man she loved, but it wasn't. I didn't blame her for that. Love is hard to forget. I did blame her for not cutting him out of her life entirely . . . though my nephew wasn't an easy husband, I'm sure of that. In these days there could have been a divorce. Then it was not possible, not to one of us. Just how far their indiscretion went I cannot say. I expect it went far enough. I almost hope it did. I know it went so far that after my nephew's death, neither of them felt they could marry. In one sense they've had their hell on earth. I'm very sure of that."

She moved her faded eyes from mine and sat for a long time looking into the fire.

"He loved her very deeply. I know that tonight more clearly than I've ever known it, and she must know it too," she said softly. "Because you see, my dear, he took two lives—how sacred those lives were I'm too near the Judgment Seat myself to say—and his own to save her."

She smoothed the heavy black faille of her full skirt with time-slow hands as I sat, just staring at her.

"The tragedy of it for me is that it was my fault. I hope God will forgive them, all three of them, and me. I was only trying, in a very stupid way, I know now, to right another wrong."

I sat there in the deepening twilight at her feet, not very sure whether I was hearing or dreaming. The firelight flickered behind us in the mirror blind with age like its mistress. She laid her hand on mine.

"Because you see, my dear, Colleton did not kill his father. His mother did it."

My hand must have carried the shock I felt to her.

"I know, my dear," she said. "It's a very terrible thing. It's more terrible, I think, to let a child grow into manhood bearing a brand he has no right to bear to save another— even his mother. I have always felt very bitterly that my niece allowed him to make that sacrifice."

"But she did so—" I began.

She shook her head.

"No one has a right to permit such a sacrifice. It was the truth of that that I wanted Jennifer to know some time. I

137

wrote it down, one day a number of years ago when Jennifer came home from school after another child had taunted her with the fact that her brother was a murderer. I wanted her to know what I knew he would never tell her—after my death and her mother's—that her brother was not a murderer."

The clock ticked slowly in the deepening silence.

"It was that paper that Phyllis Lattimer found. I had not mentioned John Michener's name. I wrote only that I was an eye-witness to the fact that it was Elsie Reid and not her son who killed my nephew. I did not say he had taxed her in front of the child with being in love with his cousin John Michener, who was leaving the plantation at the moment. Nor did I say that my nephew picked up a gun and started out to shoot John Michener, nor that his wife took up another gun, threatened to shoot, and when he did not stop, shot him dead. The men came back. There were too many of them to pretend it was an accident. Colleton, who was fifteen, took the gun from his mother's hands . . .

"When that paper came into Phyllis Lattimer's hands, she took it directly to John Michener, not knowing that he knew already that Mrs. Reid had killed her husband to save him. She wanted to destroy all of us. I think she must have been a very cruel woman. She wanted to know—from the man most nearly involved in it—how to open up a murder case that had been settled a decade ago. She wouldn't leave the paper with him. He went upstairs that night to go over it again with her, killed her, wrote me a note telling me what he had done and why, and returned the paper to me. I had already realized they were gone, and made every effort to get them back peaceably. When Jennifer brought the box back, and that paper was missing, I sent her back again. It seemed cruel, but it seemed less cruel than having her mother tried for murder."

"Did she know?" I asked.

"I thought not. I told her they were old love letters of mine. But when the note came with the paper, I had to have her read it to me to be sure. She told me then that she did know, that I needed never to have written about it. She was playing with her dolls in the next room, and saw from the door what I saw from the hall."

She sat unmoved, as cool as a spun silver thread.

"I have lived a great many years, my dear," she said quietly. "I have learned only one moral lesson. We pay dearly for every act of folly we commit. It was stupid folly that led me to write the letter I did. I know it now. It was sealed and addressed to Jennifer, to be opened only after her mother's death. It was wicked and malicious folly that led Phyllis to open it when she had no right to do so. My folly sprang from the intense bitterness I felt against Mrs. Reid, not only because of her marriage, which was folly, and her affair with John Michener, which was even greater folly, but chiefly because she had failed in courage to bear the consequence of that folly, and allowed a boy to bear it for her. All of us have suffered, bitterly . . . Phyllis Lattimer and the French woman because their folly sprang from wickedness, mine from stupidity . . . John Michener's from love."

She paused a moment.

"After all, my dear, death is the great release . . . but I am glad, and I realize now what a burden has been taken off my own soul because I am able to be glad, that Jennifer wanted to be with her mother tonight . . . for forgiveness is also a great release. And now if you will ring, I think I shall retire. I'm old, and I am tired."

I reached over and pulled the faded needlepoint bell pull. Somewhere in the silent empty reaches of the house I heard a faint silvery tinkle. In a few moments the two old colored women came.

22

I sat there alone in front of the fire, wondering what the little old lady would think if she knew the real extent of the folly that surrounded her. Mrs. Reid had paid for her husband's, would go on paying for her own. It seemed curiously ironic, I thought, that her final attempt to wash up the payments had brought the whole bitter load down on us in one great avalanche. It was almost as if she had escaped too long; in trying to destroy the illusion she herself had built for self-protection, she had unleashed the furies.

It was another instance, I supposed, of what Miss Caroline, with the euphemism of the Old South, called folly. In trying to wipe out the past Mrs. Reid had recreated it . . . a victim of her own fate, or perhaps—and I've thought of it many times, still not entirely sure in my own mind—a victim of Phyllis's fate. Whether Mrs. Reid believed Miss Caroline's memoirs were so valuable, or whether it was Phyllis who persuaded her they were, I don't know. I know only that each of them was driven to destruction by something inside her. Perhaps Miss Caroline was right. At any rate the Greeks had a word for it . . . though perhaps it's silly to say that the

Erinys could drive Phyllis and Mrs. Reid and John Michener, to say nothing of poor Felice, to destruction.

Perhaps it was because the sun was out the next morning that the old house didn't seem as desolate and forsaken as it had. As I crossed the hall into Miss Caroline's drawing room the yellow light streaming in the windows seemed to pour down a new quickening warmth there. Miss Caroline was sitting in her chair, erect, brittle and Dresden, with her old ageless quality of spun steel but softened now to a kind of gentle tenderness I'd never seen in her before. Perhaps it was that, and not the sun.

More likely, however, it was something between the two others already there, that glowed as warm and radiant as the sun. Jennifer, who had just come, was bending over her aunt's chair. Rusty, looking as if he'd been there some time, stood by the carved mantel, watching the two of them. He grinned at me.

Jennifer turned and smiled, a new softness in her blue Mediterranean eyes. Miss Caroline hadn't seen me, or heard me come in. She held Jennifer's hand in her own, so tenuous and yet so firmly gripped to life.

"There's only one thing I wish to say to you, Jennifer, and you, Rusty, now that you know all that has happened, and why. I have never blamed your mother for the one thing you think I blame her for. I want you to know that. I have never blamed her for that instant, or that impulse that meant death for your father. She killed a man she did not love to save one she did. I know I would have done the same."

Her trembling wood-wind voice paused a moment. The silence in the old room was soft as velvet.

"I believe a woman finds her own soul only when she makes a sacrifice for love."

I didn't look at Jennifer. I could look only at old Miss Caroline's faded eyes gazing back down the long avenue of years, misty with silver moss and softly mauve with entangled wisteria of forgotten dreams.

"When you two can marry here in this room I shall be very happy indeed. There is only one thing I could not have borne . . . and that, Jennifer, is why your father, for all his faults, and he was very human, will always be . . . more than I can tell you to me. He managed my business affairs—ably and devotedly. I have seen my friends suffer bitter poverty. He saved me that. That's something I could never have faced . . . seeing my home, the plantation, the furniture, the pictures, sold to the Yankees. I couldn't have lived knowing that. I thank God in my heart for your father who saved me that."

Miss Caroline raised her frail lovely old face with its wet

140

tender eyes up to Jennifer, and smiled, peaceful and confident.

Jennifer stood perfectly motionless for a moment. Then she bent down suddenly and held the little old lady in her arms, her young blue-black head pressing tight against the tiny white lace cap. Her eyes were bright with tears. It was an absolution—for her mother, not for her. She raised her head. For a moment she and Rusty Lattimer looked at each other. Then they both smiled.

www.ingramcontent.com/pod-product-compliance
Lightning Source LLC
Chambersburg PA
CBHW022028170626
46808CB00003B/1097